GUARDING JENNA

BROTHERHOOD PROTECTORS WORLD

DESIREE HOLT

Twisted Page Press LLC

Published by Twisted Page Press LLC

Edited by Wizards in Publishing LLC

Cover by Croco Designs

BROTHERHOOD PROTECTORS

ORIGINAL SERIES BY ELLE JAMES

To Jack Carr, former SEAL sniper, author of the best-selling James Reece series, and an all around incredible human being. You inspire me. Thanks for letting me steal you for my hero. I hope I did you proud.

Dear Readers,

I hope you enjoyed this, my second story for Elle James' Brotherhood Protectors. I love writing romantic suspense and creating exciting characters. But I don't do it for myself, I do it for you. And I always welcome your feedback.

This particular story is a little different because it was inspired by a real person, Jack Carr, former SEAL sniper (and now bestselling author) who I have had the pleasure and privilege of becoming friends with. I actually sent my cover artist a picture of him and asked her to find a hero for my cover that looked as close to him as possible, and she did a great job. So Jack, I wrote this to honor you for your service and for embracing our friendship.

I have a lot of help producing a book, from Margie Hager, longtime friend and beta reader to Kate Richards, terrific editor and friend, to Maria Connor, the best PA in the world. I could never do this without you guys.

I want to invite you to join the Desiree Holt Reader

Group, where we give away lots of stuff and talk about my books. So come on down.

https://www.facebook.com/groups/DesireeHoltReaderGroup/

Please visit my web site: desireeholt.com., where you can also sign up for my newsletter and clam your free book.

And finally, at the end of this story is Chapter One of *Hidden Danger,* my first story for brotherhood Protectors. Enjoy!

Desiree

CHAPTER 1

IT WAS the emails that pushed her.

Jenna Donovan had been keeping track of things online for the past fourteen years. She'd made a list of possibilities and every so often, when it wouldn't get out of her head, she did a search for anything relating to those names. She had pitiful little to show for it, but her obsession with finding the right person was like an itch she could never scratch enough.

And then the emails arrived.

There is a rapist and killer here where you used to live. He's killed ten girls in fourteen years. No one can stop him. He rapes them and then kills them if they report it. No one will help us. Please do something.

She could still feel the paralyzing shock that gripped her when she read it. Why had this person reached out to her? Did they know what had happened to her all those years ago? While she was still fighting back the nausea the memory caused, another email dropped.

We read all your stories. Please, if you can, we beg you to come investigate this or he will keep on doing it. Please.

Jesus!

Of course, it was the same man. Had to be. There wouldn't be two in such a sparsely populated area. How old would he be after all these years? And how powerful was he that he could keep doing this without retribution or discovery? The memory had slammed into her as if it had just happened. Her stomach clenched again as the nightmare she worked so hard to suppress came flooding through her as if a damn had broken.

She had run to the bathroom and vomited until her stomach was empty. Then, after settling her stomach with a cup of peppermint tea, she sat back down at her computer. She'd sworn never to return to that place where her nightmares began, but she could feel the fear rising from the messages. And she could feel the fear and desperation in the emails. Was this a sign from the universe that it was time to deal with the past? That doing one of her investigative pieces was the way to do it? Returning now was what she'd call an evil necessity. And maybe she could put her demons to rest once and for all.

Could she do it? What would it be like returning there? Who would she talk to? She had absolutely no intention of communicating with Roger Holland, her stepfather. Or former one, since her mother was now dead. It was his house—his ranch—that had been the scene of the event that still haunted her every day and night. He might not have been the actual villain, but he had created an environment that attracted people like the one in her nightmare. She'd never told him what happened, knowing he'd call her a liar. He always defended his friends in any situation, to the exclusion of everyone else, including his family.

Fourteen years ago, she hadn't been able to get away from Montana fast enough. The day she turned eighteen, she took all the money her father had left her and headed for college on the other side of the country. Despite the pleading and tears from her mother, for her own sanity she'd had to get away.

Since the day she left, she had done her best to avoid coming back here at all, the place where her nightmares began. The death of her mother in the middle of her freshman year left her without a reason to ever come back. She'd put herself through college and built a new life for herself away from any reminders of the nightmare. If she still had nightmares, well, she was dealing with them as best she could.

Putting aside everything else she had going at the moment, she did a deep search for killings in that county, going back fifteen years. And there they were, scattered over time, very brief news articles about girls who were strangled and left in the forested areas of the Crazy Mountains near her former hometown. Maybe if she went back there and helped uncover the perpetrator, her nightmares would stop forever. Maybe she could have a healthy relationship with a man. Maybe a lot of things.

"I have to go back," she told her friend, Grey Holden. "This is a sign, Grey. If I can find out who this is, maybe I can finally have some peace after all these years."

Grey had done his best to talk her out of it. Besides being her friend, he was the head of The Omega Team, a highly sought-after security and paramilitary agency, and former military himself. She still remembered the night he'd saved her from a meltdown in a bar, even though he hadn't known her from Sally Jones at the time. After that, he'd become a confidante, support person, and all around good guy in her life. But she wasn't going to take his advice on this. It was an itch she'd been waiting to scratch for a long time, one that was now almost an obsession with her. Somehow, she felt she needed to do this to get on with the rest of her life.

"Are you sure you want to follow through on this?" he asked. "Maybe you should reconsider doing the story. Going back there, digging around, is sure to bring back all those memories."

"On the other hand," she pointed out, "it may be the only way to put them to bed once and for all.

Someone went to the trouble of sending me an email, using a net café so they could be anonymous."

"But all you have," he pointed out, "are very brief articles over a fourteen-year span about the murders of some girls who reported being raped. I understand that the timing isn't exactly coincidental. They report the rape and then why're dead."

"Because that's what he threatens," she insisted. "That's what he said to me. If I opened my mouth to anyone I'd be dead meat. Murdered."

"And how did he—whoever he is—know about the complaints? Did the sheriff tell him? If they don't know his name, how would anyone know who to leak the information to?"

She bit her lip. "Somebody knows, and I want to find out who's been shielding him all these years. If he's been getting away with it all this time, it means he's a man with a great deal of power and influence. Maybe even reaching into the office of the sheriff. It's even possible he's such a powerhouse in the area that the girls or their parents confided in him, asking him what to do. It has to be something like that, because the rape complaints weren't made public."

"And you're sure these are connected? I have to ask."

She swallowed her frustration. "Yes. And whoever sent me the email said he—or she—knew for a fact it had happened to each of the girls who were murdered. I think this person knows or knew some of them, because the email described things about the rape that were never made public—big man, rough hands large enough to cover her eyes and mouth, powerful, arrogant, as if he was untouchable. And that shortly after they reported it, they were found dead. Strangled. That's what the rapist threatened me with."

"Jesus, Jenna."

"These murders have occurred over a period of several years," she reminded him. "Some of those victims would be closer to my age now, except they're dead. And who knows how many others were victims between the time I left and now? Girls who haven't ever come forward."

"And you're sure this is the same man? "

"Please." She snorted a laugh. "How many stories like this do you think come out of rural Montana, anyway? You know I never believed I was the only one this guy targeted."

"Yeah, I know. I know."

"I've been at this for a long time, Grey, and I've learned to trust my instincts. When I started looking into the murders, I couldn't believe the number of cases I found. And who knows how many rapes happened that were not reported? Like mine."

"Okay, so he killed the girls who came forward," Grey reminded her. "Even if, like you, they couldn't identify him. Even though all they had was the location and situation and sketchy information. Just on the off chance they might remember the tiniest detail. He was sending a message to all the others, right?"

"Yes, and Grey? One of them was one of the few friends I made when I lived here. Julie Kemp. At the time, I had no idea she'd been raped. She just one day stopped seeing me or anyone. When her body was found, the sheriff said it had to be a stranger in the area, but no one was ever caught. I'm still devastated about it."

"All the more reason to be cautious."

"But—"

"The person who wrote the email had to know more than one of the victims if she told you he'd warned each of them," he reminded her. "Just like he warned you what he'd do if you ever said anything."

"But that's why he keeps getting away with it," she cried. "Because he's some kind of powerful figure, ruled by his ego. He makes sure the girls are too intimidated by him to act, or he kills them. This is a habit that's gone on for several years. For whatever reason, those girls took the chance.

"And they paid with their lives," she told him, her voice tight at the thought of it.

"Let me repeat this. Because somehow word got out about what they'd done, and he made good on his threat. Of course that wasn't mentioned in any of the stories. We don't know how it leaked, so you'll` have to watch your step everywhere."

"I believe there has to be someone who knows who he is. They just keep quiet about it because it doesn't matter to them. If he's one of Roger's friends, I can tell you they'd all overlook just about anything. They all have more money and/or power than you can imagine, and they think they are untouchable. It's time for it to stop."

"You're a good reporter, Jenna," he told her. "You've won some prestigious awards for your work. You've written two very successful true-crime books. Chances are he's aware you've been digging into these cases. It's very possible he's paying someone in the sheriff's office to keep him in the loop. That's why none of the cases ever go anywhere. What if he's been keeping an eye on you all these years, especially after your awards and your very successful books? If you show up in his playground, you might as well paint a target on your back."

"Truthfully? I think he's arrogant enough to believe I have no idea who he is, or that I'll find out. Or if I do, that despite everything I'm too scared to tackle him or he's too untouchable." She blew out a breath. "Maybe if I can finally identify him and nail him, I'll have some peace myself and be able to get on with my life."

She'd been carrying this bag of heavy rocks for a long time, and she desperately wanted to get rid of it. She knew for a fact she'd never fully heal unless she did.

"You're sure he lives in that area?" he asked again.

She nodded. "I am. Believe me, I've thought about it a lot. Too much. He could have been one of the many elite of the world who flew in for the high-dollar events my stepfather liked to host, but I just have the nagging sense that he lives around there. All the girls who came forward lived in that area. And something he whispered in my ear made me think he was local. It kills me that I can't remember what it was."

She gnawed on her thumb, a bad habit she wished she could break.

Grey shook his head. "I can't say this enough times. If this guy is killing anyone who comes forward on a rape, what's to stop him from going after you? You're kicking up dirt in his playground. And no one was ever charged, with either the rapes or the killings."

"Which is why he keeps getting away with it."

He nodded. "I just want you to look at every angle here. If it's someone as powerful as you think—and I agree with you on that—he'll have his eye on every-thing and killing is obviously not a problem for him. A couple of the girls who were killed were just visi-tors in the area."

"Fresh pickings," Grey pointed out.

"It baffles me that he's still free."

"Because he leaves no evidence and kills victims

who speak out. All those cases are still open investigations."

"Going nowhere," she reminded him.

"I'll say again, he has to have an inside track somewhere. Go out there and you don't know who or what you'll be stirring up." He studied her with those eyes that could see everything. "I just wish you'd change your mind."

"Grey, someone went to the trouble of emailing me and drawing me into this. There has to be a connection. I have to follow it."

"You sure you'll be okay out there? I mean emotionally. Revisiting the scene, as they say."

"I won't be going anywhere near my stepfather's ranch," she assured him. "Hey, we haven't even exchanged two words since I left there. You can bet he was damn glad to get rid of me. Maybe he's forgotten all about me by now."

He shook his head. "How can he not even want to know what's wrong?"

She shrugged. "I'm nothing to him. I hated him from the day my mother married him. When I was thirteen, he was already looking to arrange a business marriage for me as soon as I turned eighteen. And my mother was no help at all. She couldn't understand why a marriage into wealth and status didn't appeal to me the way it did to her."

"That's something I don't understand."

"I loved my mother, but she never got over my

dad leaving her, and she was swept off her feet by a real asshole asshole. Roger Holland is arrogant, filthy rich, and travels in high society. She thrived on being the society hostess and rubbing elbows with the world's elite. He knew I hated him and, when I balked at his plans, he wrote me off. Anyway, I'm going. I found a great cabin to rent. There's a whole group of them clustered at the foothills of the Crazy Mountains. I haven't exactly broadcast my intentions, so I'm sure my target has no idea that I am trying to identify him."

"Yet."

"What?"

"He has no idea yet."

She sighed again. "Grey, I'll be fine."

"Yes, you will," he agreed, "because I'm getting you protection."

"What?" She shook her head. "No, you are not sending someone with me."

"That's right, I'm not. But I called Hank Patterson in Eagle Rock. He heads the Brotherhood Protectors. I told him what you needed, and he's assigning one of his best to you. A former SEAL named Scot Nolan. He'll be waiting when you get to your cabin."

"Grey, this man I'm trying to find, whoever he is, has no idea I'm hunting him. That I'm digging into these cases. And I'll fly well under the radar. I don't need a babysitter."

"If he's as powerful as you think, your radar won't

do you any good. And this man's a hell of a lot more than a babysitter."

"Then maybe I can smoke the asshole out."

"Not your smartest idea," Grey objected. "But if that happens, you'll definitely need protection. I take care of my friends, Jenna. Deal with it."

Jenna gritted her teeth. "If I'm walking around with a guy who might as well have a sign on him that says bodyguard, how far do you think I'll get?"

"A lot further than if you're dead. Anyway, Hank Patterson and I got it all figured out. Nolan's going to be your boyfriend."

"My—" She'd stared at him. "Oh, great. I barely hook up with anyone I know, never mind a complete stranger. No. Just no."

"Too bad. We've got it all worked out. Hank's already made the assignment, and Scot Nolan has your file so he can know as much about you as anyone else does."

"This sucks, Grey."

"Not as much as being raped again or dead," he pointed out. "Anyway, you have nothing to worry about him crossing the line. Scot's a loner. Hank says he wishes the guy would find a nice woman and settle down but, he seems to be fine by himself."

"Good, because I am, too."

So here she was, about to face her demons.

I can do this. I can definitely do this. No, I have to do this or I'll never have any peace.

She murmured the words over and over to herself as she steered her rental SUV down the highway from Bozeman to the cabin she'd rented at the foothills of the Crazy Mountains. She hadn't wanted to come back here, but if she was going to see this thing through to the end, finally, she had to do it. But she wasn't staying anywhere near Helena, that was for damn sure. Nor had she bothered to let her step-father—a man she'd hated from the day she met him—know she'd be here. That would be defeating the purpose.

Then the emails showed up, and everything came rushing back like a tidal wave, engulfing her. Thinking about it now sent memories skittering through her brain, along with the words of her therapist.

Rape is the most demeaning kind of attack. It robs the victim of...

Out of nowhere, the feel of hard masculine hands covering her eyes and mouth popped into her brain, choking her. The scent of alcohol so strong. Someone dragging her into a room, throwing her on the bed—

Choking, she swerved to the shoulder and stopped the car, slamming her hand against the steering wheel

No, no, no. I will not think of it.

Deep breaths. That's what her psychologist always told her. Take long deep breaths. Inhale. Exhale.

That's what she'd been doing for the past ten years, ever since she'd decided dealing with the aftermath by herself wasn't working.

Inhale. Exhale.

Damn. She'd thought she had the recurring images and sensations under control. She rolled down her window and drew in a deep breath of the fresh Crazy Mountains air, spiced with the essence of white birch and lodgepole pines.

Inhale. Exhale.

She felt all her inner muscles relax, the tension easing as it usually did, her breathing evening out. She closed her eyes and counted to fifty, as her therapist had told her to do, and called up pleasant images —the sun setting over the water, A child on a playground, a dog chasing a stick on the beach. After a few moments she felt calm enough to continue. She was almost there. Almost in a safe place.

And hungry. She'd either been on a plane or driving most of the day. Digging in the console, she found the last of a package of snack crackers and chowed them down. Calmer now, she put the car in Drive and pulled out onto the roadway again. It pissed her off that even after all these years, any little tiny piece of memory could still set off a panic attack. With effort she focused on the highway and the magnificent scenery on either side. The beauty of the Crazy Mountains and Yellowstone National Park should be enough to soothe anyone, right?

Then she remembered Grey's insistence on the bodyguard. Even now, she didn't know whether to laugh or scream or be grateful. She was more than grateful for Grey's friendship. He had been her rock so many times when she'd been on the edge of a meltdown. But, except for him, she had enough trouble dealing with men as it was. How would she be able to handle having one around twenty-four seven?

She was still talking to herself when she rounded a curve in the road and found herself in the little enclave of log cabins. Twenty of them. That's what the rental agent had told her, but each one far enough from the others to ensure privacy. Every porch had a number on it so she cruised slowly down the road, checking each one.

Then she realized she didn't need any number at all. A big pickup truck was parked in front of cabin fourteen, and a tall, lean man who looked as if he ate nails for breakfast stood on the porch. He was well over six feet, his dark-brown hair slightly shaggy, framing a face defined by high cheekbones and a beard that shielded his jaw.

Warrior. That was her first thought.

Her second was, *He doesn't look very friendly.* She could almost see the wall around him.

And third? Here stood the first man to ever kindle a tiny flame of desire and penetrate the ice that enclosed her body. A need that made her nipples harden and an unfamiliar throbbing set up in the heart of her sex. Oh my god! How did this happen right now, of all times, after years of failure and closing herself off? She wasn't sure she'd even know how to act. Life was playing an unfair trick on her.

Exactly how was she supposed to do this now?

Bodyguard, she reminded herself. That's what he was and all he was going to be. But she trembled nevertheless at the sudden assault of unfamiliar feelings.

Stop it! Now!

She had to keep telling herself she'd be a big disappointment to him.

She parked next to him and climbed out of the SUV, stretching a little because, between the plane and the rental vehicle, she'd been sitting a lot today.

"Hello." She managed a smile for him. *Be friendly,* she told herself. *You'll be sharing a cabin—actually everything every day—for the duration of this trip.*

But she guessed smiles were not in his repertoire because he just nodded, his face a stone mask. Then he walked down the two steps to the little parking area and held out his hand.

"Scot Nolan."

Oh, well. At least he was courteous.

"Jenna Donovan."

"I know." He shook her hand once then dropped it.

16

Inexplicably, her hand tingled from the contact and heat shot up her arm. What the hell?

He shifted his stance, moving his head slowly from left to right.

Jenna looked around, her forehead creased in a frown. She didn't see anyone near them. A little way down the road, she saw a couple with two kids climbing into a van, but they didn't seem very dangerous.

"You think someone is watching us? I'm not sure anyone even knows I'm here yet."

"Did you call the sheriff before you flew out here?"

"I did, but I didn't exactly get a warm reception."

Scot lifted one eyebrow. "What did he say?"

She nodded. "I told him I had read about the murders and wanted to get some details from him. He told me he couldn't release information in an ongoing investigation. He also wanted to know what possible interest I could have in a case way out here in the boonies."

"I'm sure you know that's pretty much standard in situations like this."

She sighed. "Yes, but I was kind of hoping I could talk him into at least sharing some information with me. He sounded more irritated than anything. Still, he did agree, grudgingly, to meet with me, after I told him I'd camp out in his lobby until he did."

"Do you want me to call Hank and see if he can put some pressure on him?"

Jenna shook her head. "No, thanks. That would only piss him off more. I'll see what he has to say to me in person. "

"He could be under a lot of pressure from a number of different factions," Scot pointed out. "Nobody outside of his office has made the connection between the rapes and the killings because no one knows about the rapes. Right? If this guy is as powerful as you think, and he's really from around here, it's possible he's got a line into the sheriff's office to bury this."

Her jaw dropped. "Bury nine rapes? Nine murders?"

Scot shrugged. "It's not unheard of. And if that's true, he probably already knows you're chasing this."

Her stomach muscles clenched. She'd thought about that but hoped she could do it under the radar. Stupid of her.

"You're right." Of course he was.

"Let's get your stuff inside."

Scot headed for her SUV. When he moved, his untucked shirt shifted, and she saw a gun tucked into the small of his back. She'd seen enough artillery doing her stories to recognize it as a Glock 19. Well! At least he had good firepower.

"I can get my stuff," she protested, pressing the fob to unlock the hatch.

"No problem. I've got it. Then we'll go over the ground rules."

Ground rules? Was she being protected or kept a prisoner.? *Thanks, Grey.*

But she could hear his voice in her head.

"Better pissed off than dead."

CHAPTER 2

WELL, this is going to be fun.

When Hank Patterson had told him his next assignment was to be as some woman's boyfriend slash bodyguard, he'd wanted to tell him no thanks. He did the hard jobs, the top level security, even the undercover assignments. But Hank explained in a quiet voice he was doing this for a very good friend of his, the woman was putting herself in a dangerous position, and he'd have a better chance of protecting her as her lover.

"We are the Brotherhood Protectors," Hank reminded him.

"As long as she understands it's only for show," he'd specified

Hank snorted a laugh. "Believe me, she's not any happier with the playacting than you are."

Not that he didn't want a woman in his life. He

did. Loneliness ate at him sometimes, but he couldn't seem to connect with the right woman. He didn't know if it was him or them. Sometimes he wondered if he'd just forgotten how to have a relationship. He'd deliberately blocked himself from anything like that so he could fully dedicate himself to the SEALs. He was one of those people who gave everything to one thing at a time. Now he wanted that one thing to be a woman, but it sure as hell couldn't be a client.

Damn!

Scot hauled the woman's gear into the cabin, despite her irritating insistence she could do it herself. Slanting a look of annoyance at him, she grabbed the messenger bag that he assumed held, among other things, her laptop, and marched into the cabin ahead of him. That gave him a good chance to get a good look at her rear.

He didn't know what he expected, but this wasn't it. Oh, sure, Hank had given him a folder with her picture and the basic facts about her and the situation, but seeing her in person was different. Maybe he'd expected a tall, boldly aggressive female who looked ready to go ten rounds with him.

Never trust your imagination.

Jenna Donovan was barely more than five feet, her jeans and sweater setting off a compact but curvy body. Dark hair fell in a mass of curls around a face whose most outstanding quality was huge hazel eyes.

At first glance, he thought, feisty, edgy and a

problem. His second impression was a lot more complicated. *I wonder what she looks like without her clothes on.*

Holy fucking shit!

He was shocked that he'd had any reaction to her at all, never mind one that involved her being naked. In the two years since he'd been out of the SEALs, he hadn't met a woman who appealed to him as anything but a brief fling. When he became a SEAL sniper, he'd made a conscious decision to shut out any emotional relationships. Being a sniper meant compressing emotions while doing the job. A lot of guys were able to do both, but apparently he wasn't wired that way. For twelve years he had lived with casual hookups, not needing anything more.

But now he'd come to realize he wanted a life, like most of the men at Brotherhood Protectors. Like Hank had found with his Sadie. But, somehow, it hadn't worked out. He began to wonder if he had a disconnect where relationships were concerned. Had he shut himself off for so long he'd lost the ability?

He rarely talked about it except to Hank, who understood his situation and told him not to give up. The right woman would walk into his life when he was least expecting her. Just like Sadie had for him. In two years, however, no woman had appealed to him for anything more than temporary.

Sometimes he wondered if there was something missing in his genetic makeup. His father had left when he was ten. Both of his brothers had joined the military as soon as they could and were still on active duty. And neither of them was in a sustained relationship. So yeah, maybe genetics. Then why did he have this continuous feeling that there was a big hole in his life?

Until today.

Until Jenna Donovan.

Right person, wrong time.

Damn!

She was a client. His protectee. Despite the fact that other members of the agency had connected that way, it violated his own personal code of conduct.

But damn! At first contact there was something about Jenna Donovan that flipped a switch that had been in the Off position for a very long time. As he took in the nicely rounded ass, the compact body, and the determined set of her shoulders, he told himself he was just assessing her to see how fast she could move in an emergency.

Yeah. Right. Bullshit.

But he wasn't going there. He had a job to do here, and he had to treat it just like a sniper assignment. No distractions. Use that famous personal discipline.

Uh huh.

Tell that to the sudden invisible connection that popped up. And worse, to unexpectedly swollen cock and aching balls.

Swallowing a sigh, he hefted her two pieces of luggage. "There are two setups for sleeping. A full bedroom downstairs and a loft upstairs. I'm putting your stuff upstairs. I'll be using the bedroom downstairs."

He waited for the argument that she wanted the downstairs bedroom. Of course.

"Wait. What?" She glared at him, hands on hips, irritation lining every inch of her body.

Yeah, there it was. And damn again. Instead of annoying him, all he could think of was how cute she looked when she was aggravated.

Of all the fucking luck. The woman he'd been waiting for walks into his life and she might as well have a big *Hands Off* sign plastered across her chest.

A body I don't need to think of except as an object to be protected. Object. Protect. Right. Still getting that body-guard thing fixed in my mind.

He just looked back at her and forced what Hank Patterson called his iron wall stare.

"I won't be much protection if someone breaks in and they can get to you before I even get downstairs. You could be dead by the time I reach you."

Her skin turned pale as she absorbed his words.

"You think whoever this is would do that? I haven't even started digging into anything here yet. How would he even know?"

"I always prepare for trouble," he told her. "Hope for the best, expect the worst." He paused. "If it's a problem for you to sleep up there, then go ahead and take the bedroom down here." He waved a hand at the two leather couches facing a rock fireplace. "I'll bunk out on one of those."

He watched the play of emotions across her face as she struggled with her options. She glanced up the open stairway, and he knew she was bothered by the openness of the sleeping setup there. He wanted to tell her she could prance around naked and it wouldn't bother him. He'd lost any interest in sex except with his hand ever since—

Quit thinking about it.

He waited for her to say something, but she just stood there, studying him as if he were an unwanted guest. Well, Hank did say someone else had made the arrangements for her. A boyfriend? A significant other? Great. Just fucking great.

"I'm concerned with your safety," he pointed out. "Just let me know what works for you."

The sigh said it all.

"Fine. I'll sleep in the loft." Her mouth curved in a tiny grin. "But no peeking."

"Trust me," he snorted. "That's at the bottom of my list. I'll get your stuff upstairs. Then we need to go over your schedule and some ground rules."

"Ground rules?"

"Yeah. There's one of those single-serving coffee makers on the counter. Go ahead and fix yourself a cup if you want."

"There are pods here?" Had the landlord provided them or Scot? Somehow she couldn't see him ambling trough a minimart laying in supplies.

"Hank's wife shopped for supplies so you wouldn't have to worry about it. If she got anything wrong, or there's something we don't have that you want, I'll be happy to take you to get it.

"Groceries?" She sounded like a parrot. His boss's wife had grocery shopped for her?

"Yeah. She figured after the long trip you might not be in the mood. Like I said, we can always get anything that's not here. So go ahead and get your coffee while I take care of your luggage.

He plunked her suitcases next to the bed, along with her messenger bag then took the stairway down two steps at a time. He saw that she'd taken him up on his suggestion and fixed a mug of coffee for herself. She stood by the big window looking out into the woods, sipping from the mug and staring out at the wilderness.

He was struck again by the electric energy that seemed to zing from her body.

Forget it, idiot. This is a job, not a date.

"You can stand there and look at me all day," she said without turning around. "But I won't change how I look. I'm still going to be a little too short, a little too chunky, and not very warm and fuzzy."

He didn't know whether to be shocked or just burst out laughing. There was nothing wrong with either her height or her body, but he didn't feel comfortable telling her that.

"First of all, I wasn't sizing you up. Second, whoever the hell told you that needs to have their eyes examined."

As soon as the words were out of his mouth, he wanted them back. He could have just said something a little more neutral. Objective. Only he seemed to have lost all his skills in that department, if indeed, he'd ever had any.

Jenna stared at him, one eyebrow cocked.

"Listen, I just meant…Never mind. How about I get my own coffee then we can sit down and go over the ground rules."

She turned, and he saw something flash in her eyes. Not anger, but maybe something close to it. Then it was gone, and her face became a mask showing nothing.

"Fine. But I have some rules of my own."

"Then let's get them out where we can look at them."

When they were sitting at the small hand-hewn polished log table, he took a moment to study her face. That definitely hadn't been anger he'd seen in her eyes. It was more like controlled fear she was doing her best to hide. Hank had given him the information on her background, but the details of the incident that had set her off in this direction were pretty sketchy.

"Grey said you'll have to get the details from her," Hank had told him. "He felt they weren't his to share. He just said she'd been a rape victim as a young girl and was now hunting the guy. He wanted us to know she's stepping into a situation where she could be in great danger. She's scared and determined, and whoever this guy is, he's apparently powerful enough to wipe her off the face of the earth without even blinking."

"And she has no idea who he is?"

"Not at all. Just that she's pretty sure he's a friend or at least an acquaintance of her stepfather. Who, by the way, she severed any relationship with ten years ago."

"Okay. I'm on it."

Now he studied her for a long second while he gathered his thoughts.

"Okay, some ground rules," he said again.

She quirked an eyebrow. "Ground rules."

"Uh huh. Like it or not, my boss, Hank Patterson, is good friends with your friend Grey Holden, and promised him we'd keep you safe. So. Again. Ground rules."

A corner of her mouth twitched. "I can hardly wait to hear this."

"Rule number one." He ticked it off on his forefinger. "You never go anywhere without me. And I mean anywhere. Even to get gas or buy groceries. Got it?"

Her mouth twitched again. "Got it."

"Every morning, you lay out your schedule for the day. If you're going someplace I haven't checked out first, I'll do a recon before I let you out of the car."

Both eyebrows hiked up. "*Let* me out of the car? Are you planning to restrain me or something?"

In spite of himself, he felt a grin teasing at the corners of his mouth. That wouldn't do. At all. He wasn't a person who smiled. Or even grinned.

"Scot?"

He blinked and realized Jenna was watching him, eyes narrowed.

"Yeah?"

"You were saying something about not letting me out of the car? Are you planning to tie me to my seat?"

"If I have to." He leaned forward. "Jenna, this is serious. From all the details Hank gave me, this guy you're hunting is a stone-cold killer. Do you by any stretch of the imagination think I am going to take the smallest chance of letting him get to you?"

She nibbled on her bottom lip, a gesture that—shock!—made his lower extremities send him signals. What the fuck? What was going on with him? Had someone else inhabited his body? Should he call Hank and tell him to send someone else?

No! This was his gig, and he was doing it. What-ever aberration this was would pass. Now. At once.

"Listen carefully," he went on. "Someone out there already knows you're digging into the past. Count on it. If that someone is as powerful as you think, he won't give a second thought to squashing you like a bug."

She stared at him for a moment then lowered her gaze to her nearly empty mug.

"Fine. I agree it's stupid to put myself in danger if I don't have to."

Thank god for that.

"Okay. Let's talk about other situations." He rose to brew another mug of coffee for himself. "Grey passed along the information that you have a list of potential suspects. Whoever this guy is, the minute he sniffs out you're here, almost any place you go in this town you'll be a target. You'll be out in the open, but he won't." He paused. "At least as far as you know. And while you're finding out who this asshole is, my job will be keeping you safe. 'Tis the ground rule."

Jenna sighed. "You're right. I know it. It's just— never mind. Have to figure out a starting point."

"This might sound crazy, after the law I tried to lay down, but I think we should go into town and see what's going on. Get a feel for things."

Jenna slid a glance at him. "You want to check out who watches me and why."

"Yes. And that's the best way to do it, since we're really flying blind here. I need to get a reading on who shows the most interest in you, overt or otherwise."

"Okay, I have a few rules myself."

Scot had to stop himself from grinning. She was just so damn cute when she was riled up like this.

Cute?

Crap. He had to stop thinking of her as anything but an inanimate object to protect. But that was damn hard to do when she'd flipped every one of his switches the minute he laid eyes on her.

"Okay, let's hear them."

She wet her lips, a gesture that made his cock want to wake up again.

Crap!

Get hold of yourself.

He was a former SEAL with a job today. That was his focus. He could damn well just push everything to the back of his mind until this job was over.

"I'll be talking to the sheriff and some other people. Please don't interrupt me when I'm doing that or give your opinion."

"No problem. That's not part of my assignment."

"Next thing. I don't do well with people just ordering me around. I like explanations for why we're doing certain things."

He nodded. "Just as long as you keep in mind that if I think we're in danger I'm not stopping to discuss it."

She nibbled on her lips again, sending his brain and his body into a spin, but then she nodded.

"Fair enough. I'll agree you're the expert there."

"What else?"

"Um, that's it. For now, I mean. But others may come up."

"I can hardly wait," he muttered. He could already sense she was walking trouble.

"Excuse me?" Fire flashed in eyes that he saw now were a sexy smoky gray.

Lord give me strength here. Why couldn't I have met her after this gig?

"I said, just let me know. I want you to feel comfortable with this."

She surprised him with a sudden grin that made a tiny dimple in one cheek flash real fast.

"I'll keep that in mind."

"So what's first on your list here? Do you have a schedule?"

"Sort of." She blew out a breath. "I spoke to the sheriff and made arrangements to meet with him tomorrow morning."

"He was agreeable to that?" Scot asked.

"I don't think he was too happy," she told him. "Having all these unsolved murders hanging over his head can't be too good for him."

"Yet he still keeps getting elected."

"Because he's part of the area elite," she explained. "And people like my stepfather like having a solid relationship with the chief law enforcement officer. Keep your friends close and your enemies, closer, as they say. This way Roger Holland and his friends could skirt the law as much as they wanted and not worry about it."

"Did he remember you?" Scot asked.

"Yes. He was the sheriff when I lived here, and he remembers me as Roger Holland's stepdaughter. People must like him since he keeps getting reelected."

Scot frowned. "Maybe he's not too happy that you might upset that apple cart by digging into these unsolved cases?"

Jenna shrugged. "I couldn't really tell over the phone. I think he knew that he wasn't going to be able to talk me out of this so he'd just make the best of it."

"Okay, what's after that?"

"I want to talk to the families of each of the murdered girls. I know, I know." She held up a hand as he opened his mouth. "They've already been questioned, probably many times. But I can often get things out of families the police can't because I come at it from a different angle."

"Yeah, I can understand that."

"After I see the sheriff, I'll start calling the families and ask to see them. I also want to take pictures of the sites where the bodies were found."

"Okay." So far so good. "We'll scope them out together."

"Scot, I—"

"First of all, remember the rules. You don't go

anywhere without me. Second. As a sniper, I spent a lot of time scoping out various sites. I might see things you don't."

She studied him for a moment. "You're right, Okay. I'll take all the help I can get. Then she threw him another curve ball. "I understand our cover here is that we're a couple. We need to talk about that."

Well, there was the heart of the mater. He hadn't given that much thought. Idiot.

"You should know that wasn't my idea," he assured her. "Hank and your friend came up with it."

"Grey told me that. I just—"

"I don't want you to feel uncomfortable with it. But just so you know. I can put on a pretty damn good act if I need to. And it seems to me the most logical situation, one that won't arouse a lot of curiosity."

"You don't think my asking questions is going to do that?"

"Yes, but I'll be a lot less threatening to people as your boyfriend than bodyguard."

"I guess you're right. Okay. We'll just figure it out as we go along."

"Works for me."

"Meanwhile, I want to get a look at the town. See what's changed in all these years. Get a feel for things."

He looked at his watch. "It's almost dinnertime. I

say we go into town, grab a booth in one of the restaurants, and see what happens."

Jenna nibbled her bottom lip and there it was again, the little zing to his cock.

Jesus!

That simple gesture made every one of his senses go on full alert. He wanted to wrap his arms around her and make her a promise that nothing would ever happen to her. That she'd be safe.

He planned to accomplish that to the best of his ability. He wanted to shelter her body with his and promise her nothing bad would ever happen.

Wait!

This is make believe, he reminded himself. A cover. A covert assignment. He wasn't really her by friend, or whatever term they were using. However, he needed to think of it to make it work.

Get your shit together. You have a job to do. Do it. Don't fuck it up and piss Hank off.

He cleared his throat. "Is that a problem?"

"What? Oh, no." She shook her head. "It's just... this is the first time I've been in this town in more than fourteen years."

"Are you worried people will recognize you?"

She shrugged. "Not exactly. To be truthful, I'm wondering if I'll recognize *him.*"

Scot frowned. "I thought you never saw him? The file I have said that first he had one hand over your eyes then when he pushed you down on the bed he wrapped some kind of cloth around your head."

"That's true. But all these years I've wondered if there would be something about him that would ring a bell. I'm so conflicted. I want to know and I don't."

"But if you don't find the answer, you'll never be able to get past it," he guessed.

"Yes. That's it. Well. No use postponing it. I came here for a purpose. Let's get on with it." She drained the last of her coffee, carried both mugs to the sink, and rinsed them. Then she turned back to face him, a determined look on her face. "I'm ready."

"Okay, then."

"I'll drive."

There went that eyebrow again.

"Don't like riding with women drivers?"

He shrugged. "I just feel comfortable handling my own wheels. Come on. Let's dip that first toe in the water."

They were silent most of the way into town, but there was an element of tension filling the air. Scot wasn't sure which of the many things it could be that generated it. At last she broke the silence.

"You probably think I'm as crazy for doing this as my friend Grey does."

"Not necessarily. I can understand why it would be important to you. But what do you think your chances are of actually identifying who this is?"

"It depends."

"On?"

She ticked off things on her fingers. "How much cooperation I get from the sheriff's office. What kind of information is in the files of the girls who were killed. Who else might be willing to talk to me."

"Don't you think you're taking a pretty big chance here?"

"Is that a question or a criticism?" she asked.

He slid a quick glance at her. She was sitting rigid n her seat, her face set in a look that was equal parts determination and irritation. He was damn sure he wasn't the first person to ask her that question.

"An information question," he answered. "I mean, if you decided you need a bodyguard, you must be worried whose comfort zone you'll nudge."

Again, she was silent. He could almost hear her brain working.

"Listen." She sighed. "Not to hurt your feelings, but this wasn't my idea. I would have been fine just coming in here by myself and doing my quiet research like I usually do."

He almost grinned. "Not to hurt *your* feelings, but if you're planning to poke a bear, you need to remember he won't hesitate to attack."

"This isn't my first rodeo, Mr. Nolan. I've done this before and not needed protection."

What was it about her that made him smile at her remarks? She was feisty. That was it. He liked feisty women.

Damn!

"But it usually isn't personal. Right?" When she didn't answer, he prodded, "Am I right?"

She huffed a sound of impatience. "Yes. You're right. It's never been personal before."

"And if the man you're after really lives here, isn't just an occasional visitor, you'd best remember he did away with those other girls. He won't hesitate to do the same with you."

She was silent for a long moment again.

"Okay. I get it. I'm just not used to having someone hanging around my neck."

"Better hanging around your neck than being hung by the neck."

He heard the gasp of an indrawn breath and gave himself an invisible smack to the head. Way to go, asshole. Try to remember that the body you are guarding is a real person, not someone sitting in a corner you can stand over with a gun.

"Don't you think if you're supposed to be my boyfriend or lover or whatever the hell it is, you should be a little nicer to me?"

"Right after you," he shot back. Man. She was a pistol, all right.

By now they were in the center of the small town, driving down Main Street—and what else would it be called, for fuck's sake. Although it was after six o'clock, people were still hurrying along the streets, some gathered at storefronts talking.

"You have anyplace special in mind?" Scot asked.

"I used to eat with my friends at a place right down that street." She pointed. "The Horseshoe."

"Still open," he commented. "And looks busy." He pulled into the parking lot next to it.

"Yes. It does."

Scot undid his seat belt then just waited. Jenna sat there, doing that sexy nibble on her thumb again, which was probably going to kill him, the man with the iron balls. She didn't seem in any hurry to get out of the vehicle, so he'd take his cue from her. He wasn't about to leave her sitting here alone, or let her walk by herself into the place.

"We can always turn around and head back to the cabin," he said at last. "Hank wasn't sure what you liked, so the stuff we stocked it with is just basics, but we can forage a meal out of it."

"No." She sat up straighter.

"You think he might be in there now? That you might recognize something about him? You said you never saw him."

"Yes. You're right. But there were certain things... something." She shook her head. "It's like it's been hiding in my subconscious all these years, and I can't bring it out."

"I've learned those things come to light when you least expect it." *And wasn't that just the damn truth.*

"Sooner rather than later would be good."

"You know, Jenna, there's always the chance he

might recognize you. Trust me. I'm very good at reading people, and I'll be checking out every single person in there. If you still want to do this, that is."

"No." She shifted in the seat to face him, determination in the set of her face. "I've never been a coward and I'm not going to start now. Let's go. And I'll remember to act as if I really like you. Try to do the same."

She unfastened her seat belt, opened the door, and slid out. Scot was beside her in an instant, holding her back while he scanned the area.

"You really think someone's hiding to ambush me? No one even knows I'm in town yet."

"Don't kid yourself. As high profile as we assume this guy to be, he's probably got his finger on the pulse of everything that happens around here. Besides, he could have kept a check on you all this time, learned what you do for a living, and is on watch to see if you show up here."

His words shook her.

"I didn't think of that."

"I know. That's why you have me. Okay, let's go."

He was right behind her as she marched to the door of the restaurant, back stiff, head high. This was her first time back in fourteen years. He could damn well protect her body, but he knew he was totally unprepared to help her through the other part of this. Acting like a lover? He wasn't sure he knew how to do it when it was for real, never kind make believe.

It wouldn't be so bad if his body would quit sending him involuntary signals. His relationships with women were all about sex. Just sex. Nothing more. He'd figured out a long time ago he might not be capable of anything more. So, what was with this unwanted reaction to this woman?

Maybe he should rethink this whole boyfriend bit he was supposed to be playing. And the term "boyfriend"? At his age? Wasn't that a little too juvenile sounding? How was he supposed to keep it to playacting when she was the first woman to flip all his switches to the On position in what seemed like forever.

Damn. Maybe Hank should have sent someone else.

CHAPTER 3

THE HORSESHOE WAS two thirds full when they walked in, the air filled with the busy hum of conversation. The restaurant hadn't changed much since the last time she'd been here, and that was nearly fifteen years ago. The same leather booths lined two walls, the same rustic tables and chairs filled the center of the place, and the same long counter stretched across one wall in front of the kitchen. She wondered how many people eating dinner now or working here remembered her. She only vaguely resembled her teenage self, so maybe no one.

Jenna spotted a booth in a corner, which was just what she'd hoped for. She wondered who might recognize her after all this time or if she could slide in under the radar. They'd be out of the way of the people who would be scoping out two strangers, at least for the most part. Hopefully, they could eat their dinner in peace.

Still, she wondered if it was her imagination that the level of sound diminished as she and Scot made their way through the room? She looked straight ahead as they moved past the tables until she could slide into the empty corner booth.

"Let me sit in that seat." Scot stopped her from sitting down in the seat against the wall.

"Why?"

"So I can have my back to the wall and can keep eyes on the entire restaurant." His mouth quirked in what she thought passed for a smile. "Besides, this way you don't have to look at anyone but me."

Unfortunately that won't be any kind of a hardship. Whose idea was this "be a couple" business, anyway, and how am I supposed to keep it playacting only, when I have this unwanted electric reaction to him?

She watched him slide into the seat opposite her with smooth, masculine grace, not even having to make an accommodation for the Glock at his back. He unzipped his hoodie, shrugged it off, and smiled at her. Sitting across from him, she took her first really good look at him, and thought, *Holy shit!* The beard was trimmed and just thick enough to give his face a hard but very sexy look. This close, she could see that his eyes were not just brown but a rich chocolate, with lashes so thick as to be sinful on a man. But looking into those eyes, she saw all the emotions absent from his facial expression. Grey had told her he was a SEAL, a sniper. What had he seen that he carried the history of it in his soul?

"Is there something wrong with my face?" He asked the question in a deep voice.

Jenna gave herself a mental shake. "No. Um, I was just—" What? Trying to see inside him? "Getting ready to skim a glance over the people in here."

"Go ahead, but be as casual as possible. And just do it once. It's easier for me from where I sit, and you can bet I'll be studying the crowd." He held up a hand as she opened her mouth. "Jenna, I've done this enough that they won't have any idea I'm doing it."

"I've done this before," she snapped, irritated. Okay, was that too kneejerk? But she wasn't an idiot, damn it. "How do you think I did research for my news stories or the books I've written?"

"Calm down, Jenna." He said the words in a low, easy tone of voice, as if comforting a high-strung animal. "I read your file. I know this isn't your first rodeo. But it's the first with a personal impact on you, and your welfare and safety are my one concern. So just let me do my job, okay? And that includes making sure I warn you about every little thing. Think about what happens if you let your guard down even a little."

A chill raced over her at his words. He was right. Her precious independence wasn't worth her life or safety.

"Okay. I got it." She sighed. "Thank you." Then she rubbed her forehead. "I guess I didn't stop to think bow depressed being back here would make me feel. I haven't had a good day since I was attacked, but at least in Florida I didn't have to be in the environment."

"And my goal is to help you get out of here as soon as possible. Get whatever interviews and research you came for and send you back to Florida."

A waitress arrived with water and menus. Pretending to read, she glanced sideways to take in as much of the place as she could see. There were several couples of varying ages, a few tables of all men and some that were groups of women or young girls. Some of the faces were vaguely familiar, but she reminded herself fourteen years had passed and people changed.

Was he here? she wondered. Calmly eating dinner and maybe choosing his next victim? Sitting across from his wife, maybe even with friends, acting like he was the most normal person in the world? How would she even know who he was, since she'd never seen his face?

She was not looking for her stepfather, that was for sure. Roger Holland had never set foot in any of the businesses in this town even though it was the closest to his vast ranch.

She and her mother never frequented the shops, either. Angela Donovan Holland, who had been more than content to spend her money in the stores where they'd lived before, now frequented only top-dollar places. A helicopter always took them into Bozeman or Helena for shopping, or sometimes for the high-fashion clothes Roger insisted she wear to New York and Los Angeles.

But that didn't mean her rapist wasn't here. Maybe the man was watching her right now, shocked to see her, eating his steak dinner while he watched her with assessing eyes.

A shiver danced along her spine, and she was suddenly cold, despite the warmth of the restaurant. Once again the memory of those hands over her eyes and her mouth, the body pressing her down into the mattress while he tied something over her face. The rough way he yanked her clothing up and pulled down her panties. She could still taste the fear in her mouth, and his threat still echoed in her head, even after all these years.

"If you say one thing to anyone I'll kill you. Count on it." Those words in a harsh whisper were engraved in her memory bank.

Her stomach cramped as she thought of the danger she was placing herself in. For the first time, she was glad that Grey had paid no attention to her bitching and that Scot Nolan was sitting across from her.

They ordered dinner, although she didn't much care what she ate. It was just to provide nutrition.

She sat back in her seat, running through her list of suspects in her brain, wondering again if she'd recognize any of them now.

"EARTH TO JENNA." Scot's voice intruded on her thoughts and dragged her back to the present.

She blinked. "Excuse me?"

He was watching her through narrowed eyes, his features set in that same implacable look. Her writer's curiosity would love to know what was behind that hard look the world saw. Was it just the things he'd seen as a SEAL sniper, or did it go deeper than that?

"I asked if you were okay. You looked like you just mentally disappeared somewhere."

"Oh. Yes, I guess so." She rubbed her face. "Just...thinking."

"Being here has to bring back a lot of unpleasant memories."

His tone of voice was surprisingly soft and empathetic. She wondered if he carried his own demons around with him. After he'd had three tours as a SEAL, the last two as a sniper, she was willing to bet there were a lot of them.

"Yes." She took a sip from the water the waitress had brought. "I thought I was prepared, but maybe that's more than I can hope for."

"You think your stepfather might show up here? I mean, just so I can be prepared."

"Not a chance." She snorted. "He never came into town. The ranch hands took care of anything he needed locally. Once I had the audacity to ask him why he'd bought this huge ranch in the middle of nowhere if he hated the place so much. He stared at me for a long time, and I could tell he was annoyed."

"Did he answer you?"

She nodded. "He said there was plenty of room to raise a big herd and still have lots of land for oil and gas drilling. He didn't need to talk to anyone around here. There's nothing they could say that would interest him."

"Sounds like an arrogant ass to me."

"No kidding." She took another sip of water. Her throat was dry, as it often was when she talked about the man. "A couple of the ranch hands were very nice to me, though. But then one of them mentioned that I was lucky to have a father who'd made so many millions from his drilling, on top of the cattle sales. Oh, and breeding his prize bull. Let me know he was practically printing money."

"Sounds like he had all his bases covered. But I wonder about a man who owns all those thousands of acres of land out in the middle of no place and doesn't make himself a part of any community."

Jenna shrugged. "My mother used to say it was perfect for entertaining, and holding high level meetings. His guests didn't seem to be bothered by the isolation. In fact, they acted as if they preferred it."

"Yeah?" He frowned. "Where did he house everyone?"

"He had several guest suites at the main house, plus he could either ferry people from Helena or Bozeman in his helicopter or they came on their own. The helicopter was what he used to send my mother and I off when she got too antsy out there in the middle of no place. Or wanted to do some shopping."

She always took me with her. Was there something she was afraid of? Did she know he had a friend who liked raping young girls? More than one friend?

The thought popped into her head, as it often did when the memory slammed at her.

Scot waited while the waitress placed their dinners in front of them before saying anything else. "Did you ever think he might be doing something illegal?"

Jenna gave a short laugh. "Oh, yeah. Even as a teenager, I didn't trust one thing about him. And I never liked any of the people who came to the ranch for his big parties, either. They were all rich assholes like him. Entitled. Arrogant. All those adjectives."

He nodded at her plate. "Let's eat before the food gets cold. I didn't mean to ruin your appetite. We can talk about the rest of this later."

Jenna wasn't sure she wanted to talk about it at

all. She'd spent so many years burying everything as deep as she could. But she knew if she were to write the story properly, it would all have to come out of her mental closet.

She'd ordered the chicken-fried steak, something she remembered as being a favorite, and had eaten about three bites when a deep voice interrupted her silence.

"Jenna Donovan?"

The voice stabbed right into her memory, and she nearly dropped her fork. Then she looked up at the tall man standing beside their booth, dressed in khaki slacks, a tan shirt, and a rancher's jacket. He had aged well, the gray at his temples making him look distinguished instead of old, the lines in his face that came both from aging and squinting at the sun giving him a decidedly masculine appearance. His body was still fit and muscular, making her wonder if he worked out to keep in shape.

The flap of his jacket shifted, and she saw the star pinned to his shirt.

The sheriff, Jeff Bartell. Of course.

Across the table, Scot set his own fork down and adjusted his position so he could be ready for whatever happened. She had to admit, it made her feel a lot better to know someone had her back, even if it was about the sheriff.

She wet her lips. "Sheriff Bartell."

His mouth quirked in a smile. "If I hadn't seen

your picture on the back of your latest book, I don't think I would have recognized you. Nice to see you again, Jenna. I didn't realize you had already arrived in town."

"I just got here a little while ago. I was planning to call you in the morning and see when you'd be available to talk to me." She glanced around and noticed that other diners were eying them. The minute they caught her eye, they looked away.

Bartell glanced over at Scot then back at Jenna, as if waiting for an introduction.

"This is Scot Nolan. He's uh, we're together." *Smooth, Jenna.*

"Oh. Well." Bartell's mouth lifted in a hint of a smile. "Nice to meet you, Nolan."

Scot just nodded, but it was obvious to Jenna he was on full alert. And in his role of boyfriend, he covered one of her hands with his and gave it a gentle squeeze. The heat of the contact shocked her as it shot through her, making her nipples tighten into hard buds and the pulse between her thighs suddenly begin to throb.

What the hell?

Get control of yourself, Jenna. Remember this is just playacting.

"So, can you spare me a few minutes tomorrow morning?" Jenna asked.

He studied her for a moment through narrowed eyes. "That's about all I can give you, but I'll tell you again, it's a waste of your time. I can't really discuss an ongoing investigation with you."

"Forgive me, but it's been ongoing for ten years. Surely by now there are things you can tell me." *Besides, I know how to ask the right questions.*

"I'm willing to discuss what's in the press release, but that's all. Is nine too early?" When she shook her head, he said, "See you then."

She wanted to ask him why, in all this time, he hadn't discovered even one clue. Had there been nothing to find, or had someone been paid off? She'd have to find a way to dig that out.

"Thank you. We'll be there."

He gave Scot another of those hard looks then nodded again, turned, and walked away.

Jenna slid a glance sideways and realized people were watching their booth. They'd kept the conversation to low tones, but still. They were strangers and objects of interest, especially with Sheriff Bartell pausing at their booth for a conversation.

"He's not too thrilled to have you come see him," Scot commented.

"No kidding."

She picked up her fork and began to eat again, although with the thought of the morning meeting front and center her appetite had fallen off. But she ate with dogged persistence, knowing she'd need her strength. She was very much aware of Scot watching her as he ate his own meal. Was he assessing her?

Thinking about tomorrow? Wondering again why she wanted to do this?

When she'd eaten as much as she could force down, she pushed her plate away and leaned back in her seat. She had just lifted her cup to take a sip of coffee when a woman, dressed in jeans and a long dark-green sweater approached the booth.

"Jenna? Jenna Donovan?"

Jenna studied her, a frown creasing her forehead. The face, framed by shoulder-length, curly dark hair, looked familiar, but she couldn't quite place her.

"Yes?"

"It's been a long time, so I'm sure you don't remember me." The woman's voice also held a familiar tone, even as tentative as it was. "It's been a long time. Becca Reiter. I used to be Becca Schultz. We hung out a bunch in high school. I, uh, read your latest book, recognized you from the photo on the back cover, and had to come over and say hello."

Jenna's brain clicked into place. Of course! One of the few girls she'd developed a tiny relationship with. Until *it* happened, and she'd withdrawn from everyone.

The woman had been a little thinner then, and her hair had been a lot longer, but now the face was familiar. She smiled at her, doing her best to conceal her surprise that the woman remembered her and approached her this way.

"Of course. And thank you for that. How

are you?"

She shrugged. "Doing okay. Married to Grant Reiter, now. He and his brother own the feed store. We have two kids."

The woman fidgeted, her gaze shifting back and forth between Jenna and Scot.

"Forgive me." Jenna dredged up her professional smile. "This is Scot Nolan. We're…together."

Which, again, she figured sounded better than calling him her boyfriend.

"Oh." Becca studied him, curiosity stamped on her face.

In high school, Jenna had never dated. Moving to the area when she was fifteen, when friendships and cliques had already been formed, she'd felt uncomfortable in the environment. Then, after *the incident,* she kept as far away from males of any age as she could.

"We've been together for a while," Jenna added, although she had no idea why.

"Very nice." Becca looked as if she wanted to say something else but couldn't figure out what.

Jenna smiled at her. "So everything's going good for you?"

"Oh, sure. Yes. It is." A pause. "Listen. Why don't we meet for coffee? Like, maybe tomorrow morning? Catch up on stuff? Get reacquainted."

Okay, there was something here more than just a social invitation. Jenna's curiosity jumped up full-blown, and her secret antenna vibrated. What was going on here? She hadn't seen the woman in fifteen years, hadn't been close to her then, and she wanted to have coffee?

"Uh, sure. Late morning okay for you?"

"Yes. That's fine." Relief spread over the other woman's features. "There's a little place out on the highway called Eagle's Nest. Remember it?"

"Vaguely, but I'll find it. You don't want to meet here in town?"

Becca shrugged. "The Eagle's Nest has great sweet rolls. I don't get them often enough."

Okay, something was really going on here.

"Okay. Is eleven good for you?"

"Yes. Yes, it is. And thanks." Relief washed over Becca's face, but then she glanced at Scot. "And, um, can you come alone?"

Okay, so this wasn't a social get together. She curved her lips in what she hoped was a warm smile.

"Scot and I do everything together." She winked. "You know how it is. "

Becca glanced again at the man lounging in the booth. "Uh, well, sure. Okay. See you then."

And she was gone, rushing as if she'd stayed too long at their booth.

Jenna looked at Scot. "That was weird."

He leaned forward and took her hand again, lifting it to dust a kiss on her knuckles. She knew it was playacting, but she couldn't decide if she was glad he was getting into the spirit of it or not. What she did know was that it sent little unfamiliar charges of electricity through her. She looked up at him and was shocked to see heat in his eyes, intense for a long moment, then gone. She wondered for a brief moment which would be more dangerous, following through with this charade or calling Grey and telling him to have his friend take Scot off her case.

"Just playing my role," he told her in a low voice. And just that fast, the heat died out. "Let's get out of here. I want you to tell me about Becca, but not where anyone can overhear us." He signaled for the check, shaking his head when she reached for her wallet. "Boyfriend always pays, remember? Hank will just add it to the tab."

She waited until they were in the pickup before asking, "What tab? I don't even know how much I'm paying for this. Grey was very vague."

Scot shrugged. "Not my area of responsibility. I just do what I'm told. Anyway, I got the feeling Hank is doing this as a favor for Grey Holden."

"Then how do you get reimbursed?"

He gave a rough chuckle. "I just turn in the receipts. Where Hank gets the money is his problem. And don't get twisted up about," he added when she started to object. "He and Grey will work it out. They can both afford it, believe me. And who pays for meals is the least of the problems here."

"I just—" She just hated taking things from

people. Letting people do things for her. She'd made a habit from the day she left the ranch to do it all herself.

"I'd much rather talk about other things. For example, I wonder how many more people around here have read either of your books? So far, the two people you've spoken to have both read them."

"That is a very interesting question." She scrunched her forehead in a frown. "I wouldn't have thought anyone around here did."

"Grey told Hank this started because you got an anonymous email telling you about girls who had been raped, reported it and then were murdered. Do you think she's the one who sent the email? She was doing her best to be friendly, but she acted like she had a tick crawling up her back."

"So you noticed it, too?"

"Hard not to. Besides, I'm trained to look for things like that. We analyze every single thing about the enemy."

Jenna blew out a breath. "It's entirely possible. Anyone who saw her tonight talking to me could just think she's saying hello to an old friend. I don't think it was her, although I could be wrong. I mean, did she act like someone who'd been raped by this guy? Besides, if she was, she'd still be too terrified to say anything."

"Maybe enough time has gone by that she's pushed it to the back of her mind," he suggested.

"She's married now, with a couple of kids. Maybe she figures this is her chance to get this guy. Or maybe she's the one who sent you the email."

"But would she approach me out in the open like that?" Jenna sighed and leaned back in her seat. "I don't know, but I'm very interested in what she wants to talk to me about. Let's find out if she has even a tiny clue who this guy is."

"Let's just be extra careful," he warned. "You're really flying blind here. You don't know who's representing the enemy and digging for information."

Jenna rubbed her temples, the leading edge of a headache just beginning to show. "I hear you."

"You still think he's a friend of your stepfather's?"

"I do. There's no other reason he'd have been at the party that night. And if that's true, you can bet he has the same sense of privilege."

"I think you're right that he lives in the area," Scot told her. "If it was a visitor of some kind, and the sheriff knows how to investigate, his visits coinciding with the deaths would raise a big red flag."

Jenna shrugged. "It seems most likely. It gives him plenty of time to choose the girls. A visitor would have to be picking one by chance, and that doesn't always work out so well."

"What about the man who attacked you? Do you think he was a visitor?"

"No, and I can't tell you why except at the time it was a feeling I had. I was sure he knew who I was, had maybe even been watching me for a while. For a long time after that, I studied every man who came to the ranch house or we ran into in town."

"I'm happy to help any way I can, just as long as you remember my first priority is keeping you safe. Anyway, we're home, and I think maybe you could use a little nightcap to settle your nerves."

"I don't know." She climbed out of the vehicle and headed toward the porch. "I've never been much of a drinker."

"I get that. I hardly drink myself."

"For me, it brings back bad memories."

"Then let's just think of it as a liquid sleeping pill, only better tasting. And you need to be able to tuck those memories away, at least for tonight." He was right behind her and opening the door before she even had her keys out. She felt the heat of him against her body, the pure masculinity of him.

"You're probably right about needing a drink, but," she pointed out, "we don't have any liquor."

He chuckled. "The people who rent out these cabins like to provide for their guests, I guess. There's a small collection of mini bottles in one of the cupboards. Hope none of their guests are alcoholics."

She giggled at the thought. "Me, too. Okay, let's see what they've got." After looking at what was available, she chose a mini bottle of Jack Daniel's. "Might as well go for the good stuff. At least I know it will help me sleep."

She filled a short glass with ice cubes and poured the whiskey over them then took a slow sip. The tension in her body began to ease at once.

Scot studied her. "Good idea?"

"Uh huh. But I think I'll take it upstairs and finish it. Maybe I can roll over, then, and sleep without dreaming."

"Hope it works." He gave her that same weird look again. "Go ahead and do whatever you need to. I'm going out on the porch for a while."

"But it's getting cold out there," she protested.

"I kind of like the cold. Spent a lot of months in heat over a hundred degrees, so this is refreshing. If I get too cold, I'll come in."

Jenna wondered what was really bothering him. Did he have nightmares about his tours of duty as a SEAL? Was he a loner because he found it easier to keep people at bay?

Quit overthinking, she told herself. *Go get ready for bed.*

She grabbed her pajamas and toiletries kit from the loft and brought everything down to the bathroom where she changed, brushed her teeth, and did whatever else she needed to. Then she climbed the stairs again and crawled into bed, where she slowly sipped the rest of the Jack Daniel's. When the glass was empty, she burrowed into the big pillows, pulled the quilt up to her shoulders, closed her eyes, and fell into what she hoped would be a dreamless sleep.

CHAPTER 4

FUCKING DAMN.

He sat in the cab of his pickup, looking down from the rugged road that wound into this part of the mountains, hidden from view as he stared at the cabin through binoculars. Of all the asshole rotten luck. And there wasn't a damn thing he could have done to prevent this. Not without exposing himself, anyway.

He'd hope the information about her coming back here to do a story was someone's imagination. But no. Hell, no. She'd shown up wearing her investigative reporter/author personality, and now she was about to dig into history—too many years of it—and cause him a lot of trouble.

He'd been so sure he'd scared her off all those years ago. She'd trembled beneath him when he'd held her down on the bed, too frightened to scream when at last he moved his hand from her mouth. In the rough whisper that disguised his voice he'd told her exactly what he would do to her if she ever breathed a word of this to anyone. Not that they'd believe her. After all, he was a man of power and position, and she was just a snotty little brat.

Then he'd whispered every single thing he was going to do to her, how he was going to penetrate her, take her virginity, fill her tight little passage with his cock. When he thrust inside her, and she choked on her screams, he got hotter than a pistol and came so hard his body shook.

His mouth twisted in an evil smile at the memory. He lusted after snotty little brats. Even the slightly older ones appealed to him, as long as they weren't *that* old. But the virgins were the best. They got him harder than any others. Too bad they were getting more and more difficult to find. What was wrong with them that they were having sex younger and younger these days?

But that wasn't his problem at the moment. No, his biggest challenge was what to do about Jenna Fucking Donovan. He'd have to get rid of her. No question there. But he had to do it in a way that looked like an accident, one that no one would question. Once she was gone, things would return to normal. And he'd make fucking damn sure that the tasty little tidbits knew if they didn't keep their mouths shut they'd be dead meat like the others he'd disposed of. So what if they couldn't identify him? Too many reports and there'd be no shutting the door on them.

From now on, he'd bury the bodies so well they'd never be found. And then he'd remind fresh meat that it could happen to them if they ever opened their mouths. He should have hidden the bodies to begin with, but he'd thought he was sending a message. Apparently not.

The rush he got from these young girls was beyond anything he'd ever imagined. His cock was hard as a post the moment he grabbed them and threw them down. It was always more arousing, more exciting, when he did it at something like a party at Roger Holland's sprawling mansion of a ranch house. All that power, that he was part of, and none of them knew what he was doing, hidden in one of the rooms.

Certainly, his wife was unaware. As long as he was attentive to her, she'd never suspect a thing. Her needs and desires had diminished as she'd gotten older, so now he had the best of both worlds—a wife that required very little servicing and a smorgasbord of young flesh for the ravishing.

Sitting here thinking about it all made his cock swell so much it hurt, and his balls ached. He unzipped his fly, pushed the fabric of his slacks to the side, and took himself in hand. Leaning against the back of the seat, he closed his eyes, called up the image of the last piece of young meat he'd had, and stroked himself hard and fast. As aroused as he was, it didn't take him long before the familiar tingle crawled up his spine, his muscles tightened, and he exploded all over his hand. His shaft pulsed again and again, with spasm after spasm, until he had emptied himself.

He sat there in the dark for a long time, spent, catching his breath, holding his now soft dick, waiting for his breathing to slow down.

Finally, he cleaned himself up with his handkerchief, tucked his now limp shaft back into his pants, and let out a long breath. Then he looked out the window and down at the cabin in question. In the moonlight, he could make out the figure of the guy Jenna was with sitting on a bench on the porch, leaned back, feet up on the rail. Who the fuck was this guy, and how much trouble would he be?

Okay, tomorrow he'd check into everything. Find out—very carefully—how much Jenna knew and what her plans were, and who the man was. Definitely who the man was and how much trouble he could cause. After that he could figure out what his next steps would be. He needed to shut this down now, and do it in a way that would not generate even more questions. No girls had come forward since the last body was discovered, and that was two years ago. Things were nice and quiet. Settled down.

Putting his vehicle in gear he turned and headed back down the mountain.

NIGHTS WERE OFTEN difficult for Scot. Even after two years, scenes and images he'd never forget played over and over in his brain. He'd learned to sleep in short stints, just long enough to recharge his batteries but not so long that the images he wanted to shut out had their turn in his mind.

He'd sat out on the porch until the moon reached its zenith in the sky, listening to the night noises and enjoying the solitude. Although there were other cabins around, they had been placed so each one seemed to be by itself. That was good. He was okay with people but better off without them.

When his watch showed midnight, he went back inside, ready to crawl into bed for a few hours. He had just stripped down to the sweats he slept in when he heard a noise from the loft. He wasn't sure if he was just hearing something, so he waited a moment. Then he heard it again. A thunk, as if Jenna had fallen out of bed. Then he heard her talking, but there was no one up there for her to talk to.

There wasn't another soul in the cabin. He could attest to that. Should he just leave her alone? She might not welcome his intrusion into whatever nightmare she was having. They were, after all, strangers. But when she screamed, a soft but tortured sound, he knew he couldn't leave it alone.

He took the stairs to the loft two at a time. The lamps were off, but moonlight shafted in through the window, giving him enough light to see what was happening. Clad in pajama pants and a T-shirt four times too big for her, Jenna was on the floor, curled up in a ball, head tucked into her arms, and crying softly.

Something pierced his heart. He was overcome with the unfamiliar sensation of wanting to wrap his arms around her and wasn't sure what to do. Comforting people wasn't high on his personal-skills list, but the sounds she was making slapped at his heart. And the way she curled into a ball as if protecting herself. Damn! Although Hank had given him just the bare details of the rape all those years ago, he was sure none of them could truly imagine the brutality of the attack on a young girl.

While he stood there wondering if he should touch her or not, a low keening sound issued from her mouth, a sound so tortured it cut right into him.

Okay, Nolan, suck it up. Pretend she's one of the victims you helped in the sandbox.

He wasn't much good at this but right now he didn't have a choice. He couldn't just walk away and leave her like this. He crouched down beside her and with a gentle touch, pressed a hand to her shoulder.

She jerked and cried out.

"Ssh, ssh, ssh," he soothed. "It's me, Jenna. Scot. I'm not him. You're safe with me."

She rolled to her knees and began flailing at him, pounding her fists on his chest and crying, "No, no, no. Please, no."

Damn.

He sat down on the floor next to her, gritted his teeth, and grabbed her arms. Although she fought him, he pulled her body against his chest and held her until she stopped struggling, stroking her back.

"It's me. Scot," he repeated. "Hush, now. You're safe."

He rocked her against him, arms wrapped around her, crooning softly until he felt the tension ease from her body. It was then he realized with a start how intimately he was holding her. Her breasts were soft against the hard wall of his chest, her nicely rounded ass resting on one of his hard thighs.

His thigh wasn't the only thing hard, either. Not with this warm, soft body bearing the scent of some kind of flowers nestled in his arms. Well, fuck all. Why was it that the first woman who made him think he might have found what he was looking for had to have a big keep away sign on her because she was a client? His protectee? Between unlocking his battered heart and making his libido explode, he was in big trouble here.

Damn it, she was going through her own emotional crisis. She didn't need him complicating things. But hell. Holding her tight to his body, arms wrapped around her, her face soft as it pressed the stubble of his chin—for a long moment, he could forget he was a bodyguard, forget everything except he wanted her, pure and simple. And not just for a roll in the hay, like other women he'd been with in the past two years.

Didn't that just fuck all.

Her sobs had slowed to almost nothing by now, but still she sat curled into him, hands touching his bare chest, the silk of her hair tickling his chin. If only he had an ice cube to drop on his over-eager cock that had chosen absolutely the wrong time to come out and play. Using every bit of his mental discipline, he just sat and rocked her while her sobs slowed, diminished, then stopped altogether.

She looked up at him, eyes not quite focused as if she wasn't sure where she was. When she realized he was holding her, she pushed as hard as she could and scuttled away from him. Her heart pounded like a jackhammer.

"Scot?"

He saw the naked fear in her eyes and released her at once. Based on what he'd learned from Hank, he was pretty sure what her nightmare had been about.

And his hands on her weren't going to make her feel safe at all. Quite the contrary.

"In the flesh." He gave her what he hoped was a reassuring smile.

"W-what? What's happening?" She wrapped her arms around herself, and a visible shudder ran through her body. "Oh my god. What did I do?"

He spoke to her in a low, nonthreatening tone of voice. "I, uh, heard you cry out then there was a thump. I came up to see if you were okay. Looked like you fell out of bed and were trying to hide from something." He paused. "Or someone."

"Oh god." She looked down at the floor. "I must have had the dream again."

"The dream?" He had to ask, although he was pretty sure he knew what she was talking about. Along with the other information Hank had passed along was a note that she still had recurring night-mares about the rape. He was pretty damn sure that no matter how much time passed, no matter how a person tried to bury the memories, they were always lurking at the edge of the subconscious.

"I had a nightmare about…it. Again." She shud-dered again. "He was coming after me, and I couldn't run away from him. He grabbed me and— Oh god."

Okay, what was he supposed to say here?

"Does this happen a lot?" He at least wanted to be prepared.

"No." She shook her head. "I haven't had one for a long time."

"Coming back here to dig into this mess probably triggered it."

"I'm sure you're right."

He probably should get them both off the floor, but he wasn't sure if he should touch her or not. But sitting here like this, remembering how she felt in his arms, however briefly, made him feel things absent from his life for a very long time. She was smaller than most of the women he'd been with, although probably tougher inside. And while most perfumes didn't affect him one way or the other, that scent of wildflowers was driving him crazy.

It wasn't just his emotions in trouble, either. He was doing his best to send a message to his throbbing cock and his aching balls that this was all very inappropriate. It appeared, however, that his body was ignoring him.

Fuck a duck.

"I—I think I'm okay now." Her tiny laugh had just a touch of hysteria to it. "I don't usually end up in someone's lap when this happens."

"No problem," he assured her. And what did it say about him that he was glad no one else had comforted her like this. "No problem at all.

And still, neither of them moved. At last, after what seemed like a long time, she sighed, letting out a long, slow breath.

"I should probably get back in bed and let you do the same."

"It's okay. I don't need that much sleep." He had his own nightmares to deal with.

"But still." She raked her fingers through her hair. "I try not to be this much of a mess most of the time."

"Jenna." He realized he was stroking her back again. "You're not a mess. You were a victim of a brutal attack. Rape is personally destructive at any age, but to a young teen it is even more devastating. Cut yourself a break." He paused. "Is there anything I can do for you?"

She looked at him, the memory of that horrific event still visible in her eyes.

"Uh, no. That's okay." She managed a tiny grin. "Thank you for this."

"Anytime." He rose and held out a hand to her, relieved that she accepted it.

They stood there, just looking at each other for a moment, every inappropriate word running through his brain. He didn't know who made the first move, probably him because he had to lean down. But one minute they were staring at each other, and the next his mouth was on hers.

The first thought that hit him was her lips were the softest, sweetest he'd ever touched. He couldn't help using the tip of his tongue to trace a line over them. The second was that just this touch wouldn't be enough. He realized Jenna had slipped her hands down from his shoulders in a slow movement and was gripping his biceps, her strong fingers digging into his muscles.

He lifted his hands to cradle her face and slipped his tongue inside her sweet mouth. God! She tasted just the way he thought she would, sweet and sexy at the same time. He licked every bit of the tasty flesh, sweeping his tongue over hers, punctuating it with gentle bites. Her taste filled all the empty corners of his soul, all the places in his heart that were empty.

A moan drifted on the air, and he wasn't sure which of them it came from, but the sound pierced the fog in his brain. He lifted his head and stared down at her, at the sight of her lips wet and shiny and the pulse beating at the hollow of her throat.

Then, as if realizing what had happened, she almost jumped away from him. She was the first to speak.

"This didn't happen." Her voice was hoarse and unsteady. "It can't."

Scot blew out a breath. "You're right, and I'm sorry. This was very inappropriate of me."

Jenna shook her head. "That's not it. And it was my fault, too."

"I shouldn't—"

"I appreciate you checking on me and not washing your hands of me because I'm such a psychotic mess. I—" She took a step back and lowered her gaze. "I have—problems. Because of what happened. Even if this wasn't a business arrangement, I have nothing to give anyone. I'm frozen inside."

"Jenna, listen. I—"

"That's another reason why that kiss can't mean anything. I'm sorry if you got the idea that it did."

Oh, he had more than an idea. And he knew, despite what she said, she'd been just as affected by it as he was, but he'd play this by the rules. Had to.

"I take full responsibility for letting this get out of hand. If you want me to call Hank and have him send someone else, I'll do it right now."

He waited, tense, for her answer. He knew the smartest move would be to do just that, but his stupid brain hoped she'd say no.

She nibbled for a moment on her sexy lower lip then shook her head.

"No. Stay. I don't want to have to start with someone new, and you've already seen me at my worst, plus we've been seen n town together. Let's just move forward and agree this won't happen again." Her mouth curved in a weak smile. "And I'll do my best not to have any more nightmares."

"Will you be okay for the rest of the night?"

She shrugged. "Who knows? I'll try not to scare you again, though."

"I'm fine. And Jenna? Everything else aside, I'm here for whatever you need, not just protection from the bad guys."

"Thank you."

"See you in the morning."

He jogged down the stairs, mentally slapping himself upside the head.

I'm here for whatever you need?

Asshole. She doesn't need you pawing all over her.

He stepped out onto the front porch for a minute, hoping the chilly night air would cool his brain and his body and knock some sense into him. He just hoped to god she never mentioned this to her friend Grey Holden. Who would, of course, tell Hank. And then where would he be?

WHAT ON EARTH was I thinking?

Jenna thought maybe if she banged her head against the wall she could knock some sense into it. Kissing Scot Nolan? Holy shit! She didn't go around kissing men. She hardly had a sex life, as a matter of fact. Despite years of therapy, the moment a situation with a man began to hint of intimacy, she froze. The brutality of the rape and the remnants of the terror that never left her made her sex life almost nonexistent.

Not that she hadn't tried. Sometimes she just apologized and walked away. Other times she didn't have the chance. The guy just took a hike, asking her if she ever planned to loosen up and live a little.

Maybe if she'd met someone who wanted something besides sex and a good time, someone who cared enough about her to coax away the horrific memories and replace them with good ones, it might have helped. She knew it would take someone with patience to get her past this problem, but she hadn't met anyone yet who could fill that spot or, truth be told, anyone she *wanted* to fill it.

So, what? I want Scot Nolan to be the one?

Stupid. Stupid, stupid. She knew the guy for five minutes and she…what? Wanted to jump in bed with him? Have him fix her problem?

He was her bodyguard for heaven's sake.

But she couldn't erase the memory of his touch when he soothed her, the strength yet tenderness in his hands. The kiss that rocked her clear down to her socks, if she wore any. The sensitivity was the last thing she'd expected from him, the poster boy for macho man. And now she couldn't get it out of her mind.

I should have asked Grey more about this man.

But he just seemed so closed off, she'd never have expected him to do what he did. She remembered her first impression of him when she'd seen him on the porch waiting for her, that of a remote warrior. It didn't fit at all with what he had just done or what had happened between the two of them.

It was just a kiss, for the love of god. Get over yourself already.

She climbed back into bed, still wound up tight as a drum, sure she'd never get a minute's sleep for the rest of the night. But somehow she closed her eyes, and when she opened them again, sunlight was streaming in through the high window. Amazingly, she'd made it through the rest of the night.

But what would the day ahead bring?

CHAPTER 5

WHEN JENNA MADE it into the kitchen, she was surprised Scot wasn't there. The door to the bedroom was open, and she could see the room was empty. Had he gone somewhere without even leaving her a note? That didn't seem very likely. She glanced out the big living room window and saw both her car and his truck still parked in front of the cabin. Maybe he'd gone for a run. She'd learned through Grey that the majority of men who had been in the service liked to keep in shape after they got out. Grey himself got up at five-thirty every morning to run five miles before heading to the office.

Oh, well, he'd turn up soon. She knew she wouldn't be going anywhere without him. Scot's ground rules.

With a mental shrug, she set about fixing a mug of coffee. She had just taken her first sip when the front door opened and the man himself walked in. It was hard for her not to notice the way his faded jeans clung to his legs and hips or how the long-sleeved T-shirt fit snugly over his well-muscled torso.

The minute they locked gazes, an electric charge sizzled through the room. Her body seemed to be disconnected from her brain because her nipples hardened and a pulse low in her body set up a silent drumbeat.

She wondered if Scot would say anything about what a hot mess she was last night. Or mention the kiss. The damn kiss. For an unbelievable moment, she was sure she could still taste his mouth on hers. How absurd was that, anyway? This wasn't a movie where the handsome prince swoops in to save the beautiful princess by vanquishing the evil monster. There was no royalty in this room, and it was far from a movie. All it took was one look at Scot Nolan to blow that out of her brain. Whatever sizzle there was, either he wasn't feeling it or he was ignoring it.

His features were set in that same implacable look she'd noticed the first time she saw him yesterday, and his eyes had the same flinty look. Last night's version of Scot Nolan might as well not have existed.

Okay, then. That would make it a lot easier. She hoped.

"Out seeing the countryside?" she asked, just to make conversation.

"Checking something out." He headed for the coffee machine.

"Checking what?"

She waited for more of an explanation and had to bite her tongue until he had filled his mug and turned back to her.

"Don't freak out, but I think someone was watching this cabin last night."

Don't freak? Was he kidding?

"What makes you think that?" She was proud her voice was so steady and the hands cradling her mug didn't shake.

"I've learned to trust my senses. I didn't want to bring it up last night, what with…the situation."

She was sure her freak out and the kiss were what he referred to. She took a sip of coffee.

"I can understand that."

"So, this morning I just took a little stroll down the road to see if another cabin had a view of us, maybe where the road curves behind us. But whoever built these cabins did a great job. Each one sits in its own little isolated pocket."

"So, then where? Who?"

"As to where, I think from one of the narrow road cut into the particular mountain in our view. As to who, I'd be damn surprised if it was anyone but the object of your investigation."

For a moment, she was afraid the coffee she'd drunk would come right back up, so she swallowed hard, determined not to embarrass herself any more than she already had.

"So you think he knows I'm here?" *Yes, dummy. Otherwise why spy on you?* "I haven't broadcast it around. The only person I've spoken to is Sheriff Bartell." Then she shook her head. "No, the word must be out somehow. Becca Reiter wants to meet me at eleven about something she doesn't want others to know. I'll bet my next royalty check it's about this."

"And if she knows, others probably do," Scot pointed out.

"So what do I do?"

"You do exactly what you came here to do. I'm going to call Hank and have him do some nosing around in a way that won't trip any switches."

Jenna's stomach knotted. She had been so sure she could come in here and fly under the radar. She knew whoever this was had to be very rich and very powerful. If not for Scot, she was sure he could make her disappear without a trace. For the first time, she realized how right Grey had been to set this up for her. What she was setting out to do was personal for the man who had raped her and the others, and he'd do whatever it took to stop her.

"So, now what?" she asked.

"So, now we eat something, go see the sheriff and then have your meeting with Becca."

Jenna shook her head. "I don't think I could swallow food."

"You have to eat something. You can't fight stress on an empty stomach."

"Toast." She blew out a breath. "I can eat some toast. And I am more than capable of making it. But thank you."

While she munched on a solitary slice of toast, Scot wolfed down two muffins with his coffee.

"The shape you're in, I'd think muffins were off your food list."

He grinned. An actual smile. "They're my weakness. I just work out an extra hour and run an extra five miles."

It tired her just thinking about it. She rinsed out her coffee mug, set it on the countertop, and picked up her purse and her tablet. "Ready whenever you are."

He nodded.

As they rode into town, Jenna wondered if Scot was aware of the sexual tension riding in the cab with them. They might both have their reasons for vowing to ignore last night's episode, especially that damn kiss. But if they were both honest, there was definitely something there, and it wasn't going away just because they declared it would.

They were almost to town when Scot broke the silence.

"If you're meeting your friend at eleven, will that give you enough time with the sheriff?"

"I'm pretty sure it will. I'll want to go through all the reports and then talk to him again."

"I don't think the sheriff is going to give me more than the bare minimum of time it takes to get rid of me."

"You think he's trying to hide something?"

She'd had that thought and hoped that wasn't the truth. Owen Bartell had been sheriff since before her mother had married Roger Holden and they'd moved to this area. From everything she'd checked into, he had a reputation as a good lawman and was well respected. Of course, from the many stories she'd written, she knew that didn't always mean anything.

"Jenna?" Scot's voice pierced her thoughts.

She gave herself a mental shake. "No. Well, maybe, but not for himself. He might know who it is. Or think he does."

"He could be sanitizing those reports to protect whoever it is," Scot pointed out.

"I guess I'll just have to wait and see. Anyway, here we are."

The office of the county sheriff was a squat stone building that took up half of the block where it sat.

"Lot of room for an office," Scot commented as they climbed out of his truck.

"That's because the jail is attached to it. I guess when they built it they figured it was cheaper to do it all in one." She stopped for a moment, took in a deep breath, and let it out slowly. "Okay, I'm ready."

Again he checked the area, keeping her behind him, before he stepped aside so she could move forward.

She looked at him with raised eyebrows. "You think he'd try to get me at the sheriff's office?"

"Just not taking any chances, remember?

They stepped through the front door into a small reception area. Jenna tapped on the window to let the woman behind it know she was there.

"Jenna Donovan to see Sheriff Bartell. He's expecting me."

"I'll let him know you're here." She frowned. "You look a little familiar to me. Didn't you used to live somewhere around here a long time ago?"

"Yes. I did." She stepped away from the window before the woman could ask her any more questions.

"She must have a sharp eye," Scot murmured in a low voice. "You haven't been back here in fourteen years.

"I know. And when Becca came over to our booth last night, I was startled that she recognized me."

"I'll go back to something I said last night. I wonder how many other people around here have read either of your books?"

Before she could answer him, the inner door opened and Jeff Bartell's big body filled the space.

"Come in, Jenna. Let's get this over with."

After acknowledging Scot with a brief nod, he stood aside so they could walk inside. As they followed the sheriff to his office in a far corner, Jenna noticed a small office on the right shared by the secretary and a man she thought might be the under-sheriff. To the right, a larger office was filled with desks, about half of them currently occupied by deputies. Beyond that, an open space with more desks, a setup for dispatch and, on the far wall, doors leading to a couple of other rooms.

Jeff Bartell held the door to his office open so they could precede him then closed it and moved to sit behind his desk. He gestured Jenna and Scot to the two wooden chairs opposite it then picked up a folder on his desk and placed it in front of him.

"I want you to know right off the bat that the only thing I can give you is a copy of the press release we issued. Nothing else. These are all still open cases."

Jenna crossed her legs and sat up straight in the chair. "I'll take whatever you can give me. And I'd hoped you might answer just a question or two for me."

"Why are you so interested in this particular situation? We're pretty isolated out here, not a lot of traffic, not a lot of media interest. I'd like to know what turned you onto this case—or cases—and brought you all the way out here from the other side of the country. Or what made you even look for them. I read the two books you wrote as well as a couple of your more well-known stories. Usually you focus on crime in the major cities, so what caught your attention? We're not exactly a thriving population center here, nor is it like we hit the big time news outlets."

Jenna worded her response very carefully.

"Every so often I scan the Internet for little tidbits." She wasn't going to tell him about the email. "Natural reporter's curiosity. And sometimes I'll plug in the name of this county. When the items about the murders popped up, and there were so many of them, of course I was interested. I lived here for four years. Remember?"

"Of course I remember." He scowled at her. "But I also recall you didn't exactly make yourself a member of the community."

"That doesn't mean my interest isn't piqued about this whole thing. A string of unsolved murders would juice up any reporter's curiosity. I'm hoping you can at least answer a few questions for me. I mean, over and above the press release."

He didn't return her smile, just studied her again for a very long moment, as if trying to decide whether or not he liked her answer.

"I'm sure you know that's not how it goes," he told her. "We have to proceed very carefully with these cases. Besides, we don't even know if these deaths are connected. They span a few years."

"I'm going to assume you did your job and checked all likely suspects, so I ask you. Is there any reason for you to think they're not connected? I read that they were all murdered the same way and found in similar situations."

"That's true," he agreed, "but I'd hate for you to take anything I say, jump to a wrong conclusion, and throw a monkey wrench into the whole thing."

She chose her next words with great care, but she wanted to see what kind of reaction she could shock out of him. "The wrong conclusion being that all of these girls were raped, probably by the same man? And murdered after they filed a complaint?"

"Rape?" The sheriff's face paled. "What the fuck? How did you— Who told you that?"

"A little birdie. But I'm right, aren't I."

A muscle worked in Bartell's jaw. "Maybe I won't be giving you a copy of the press release after all. Can't have you stirring up this town with lies."

She leaned forward. "They aren't lies, and I'm sure you damn well know that. Someone's getting away with a heinous crime here, Sheriff, over and over again. And how many girls do you think were raped who've never come forward?"

He leaned forward. "We worked damn fucking hard to keep those complaints under the table. I wanted to be sure we did a thorough investigation before we accused someone of such a heinous crime."

Jenna gave a ladylike snort. "And how's that working out for you? Got any clues? Did you just think it was a coincidence that soon after a girl filed a report with you, she was killed?"

"Of course I didn't." He slammed his fist on the desk. "I've been working the murders hoping they would let me backtrack to who the killer is."

"And ultimately the rapist? But you've got nothing so far, right?" She blew out a breath. "Look, Sheriff. I'm not going away. This story is important to me for personal reasons. I really don't want to butt heads with you over this if I don't have to. I've done this enough before that I know how to be discreet and when to keep my mouth shut."

"I checked you out with the news services and your publisher. They all gave you high marks for discretion, so I'm going to break my own rule here." He rubbed his jaw. "I don't know how you came to know about the rapes, but I'm asking you to give me your word that you won't go blabbing about it to anyone while you're out asking your questions. I want your word on that."

She nodded. "You have it."

"Okay." He blew out a breath. "One of the reasons we haven't moved forward more on the rape charges is the girls were unable to give much of a description of the guy. They didn't lay eyes on him. All they could tell me was he was a big man. That could fit a hundred men around here."

"I'm planning to talk to the parents," Jenna told

him. "See if maybe any of the girls said something that's lodged in their memories."

He scowled at her. "You really think it's a good idea to dredge all that up with these poor people? Isn't what they have to live with bad enough?"

Jenna bit back the retort that threatened to pop out of her mouth.

"I assure you, I can be very discreet and sensitive. And I certainly won't do anything to impede your investigation." She emphasized the last word.

Anger sparked in his eyes. "Are you implying that I'm not doing my job?"

"I'm not implying anything. But it seems a little baffling that nine murders that are exact duplicates of each other haven't been solved in all these years, and that it's highly likely whoever this is continues to commit rape unheeded."

Bartell leaned forward, a muscle twitching in his jaw. "You'd best be very careful what you do out there, missy. You're right. This is a dangerous man. You don't want to poke him too hard."

"Are you worried I might uncover something while I work on this story?"

"If you do," he said in a hard, uninflected voice, "I expect you to bring it to me at once and not share it with anyone." He narrowed his eyes at Scot. "And what's with him?"

"Scot and I are a couple." She was proud she didn't stumble over the words. "I trust him with anything and everything." With my life, she thought. "And he'll make sure nothing happens to me."

Bartell studied both of them for a long moment.

"Fine." He slid a sheet of paper from the folder and handed it across the desk to her.

Jenna studied it. There wasn't much more than he'd already told her, and certainly no mention of the rape. There was, however, a very brief description of the condition of the bodies when they were discovered. Jenna made a mental note to study that later. She slid the sheet of paper into her messenger bag and rose from the chair.

"Thank you." She held out her hand. "I appreciate the time."

The sheriff stood, also. His handshake was firm.

"Don't make me regret it, okay? I'd hate to ask you to leave town because you said or did the wrong thing."

What a jackass.

"I can promise you that won't happen. And if I learn anything, I'll bring it right to you."

"Fine."

The two men shook hands then Jenna followed Scot through the offices and out to the parking lot. It wasn't until they were out on the street and headed away from the building that she breathed a sigh of relief.

"Well! That was some meeting."

"Sheriff Bartell is so uptight he almost vibrates," Scot commented.

"You're right," she agreed. "I wish I knew whether it's because he has nine unsolved homicides on his desk and people probably screaming for his head. Or because he's somehow involved and worried I'll ferret it out. I have the feeling he's protecting someone, don't you?"

"Yes. Probably whoever quietly bankrolls his elections and keeps him in office. Let's go see what your friend Becca has to say. Maybe she can shed some light on this."

"Maybe. Let's hope so. Otherwise, I've got a long haul to dig anything out."

CHAPTER 6

THE EAGLE'S NEST was about fifteen minutes outside the little town, a fairly large, square building set in the middle of a big parking lot. The lot was more than half full, mostly with pickup trucks and semis.

"Typical truck stop," Jenna commented.

"Looks like it," Scot agreed. He pulled into a spot at the side of the building, turned off the engine, and faced Jenna. "You ready for this?"

She nodded. "I think so. I guess I'm still in shock that she approached me the way she did. We hardly had anything to do with each other when I lived here. I didn't even go to my high school graduation."

"You really withdrew after you were attacked," he guessed.

"I did. I had no one I could talk to. My mother was so high on Roger and the lifestyle, and petrified I'd do something to upset it. I went to classes, kept my head down, studied and then got the hell out of here."

He surprised her by sliding his hand over her shoulders and rubbing her neck. The tingles left by his touch shot straight to her core, enough that she had to squeeze her thighs together. She slid a glance at Scot, wondering if he noticed, and saw his gaze was fixed on her thighs. Oh, yeah He noticed.

How was it possible that after all these years, after never being able to respond properly to a man in bed, after feeling that sex was a torture to be endured rather than enjoyed… How was it possible that just a simple touch from this man set her crazy hormones dances and her body heating up.

When she looked at him again, he was staring straight at her, those dark-chocolate eyes glinting with heat. What the hell was going on here?

He leaned toward her just a fraction, as if he was going to kiss her, then shifted back into his seat and opened his door.

"Better not keep Becca waiting."

As soon as she was out of the truck he came around and took her hand in his.

"Couple stuff," he reminded her, as she looked up at him. "In case anyone's watching us." Then he threw her off balance by winking.

What was it with this man that just a simple glance from him brought responses from her frozen body that she'd never had before? As they walked into the Eagle's Nest, she was glad she had a thin jacket on. It could cover her nipples, which felt as hard as rocks and were probably poking through her sweater. When they got back to the cabin, she might have to hide in the loft for the rest of the day.

The inside of the restaurant/truck stop was warm, and the air was redolent with the aroma of cinnamon and sugar. She remembered at once what Becca had said about their special sweet rolls, and her mouth watered.

The place was about half full, most of the counter stools occupied. She looked around and finally spotted Becca in a booth in a corner, similar to where she and Scot had sat the night before. Was Becca hiding, too?

They made their way to the booth and slid onto the bench across from her. Scot made sure she was on the inside, protected by his body. She half expected him to ask Becca if they could change sides. A waitress was there almost at once, with a carafe and two thick ceramic mugs.

"If you want decaf, I gotta go back in the kitchen and get it," she told them

"No." Scot smiled at her. "We're good. But bring us some of those sweet rolls, okay?"

"You got it." She scurried away

Becca looked across the table at Jenna, the half-smile on her lips belying the frightened look in her eyes.

"Thank you for coming," she said, clutching her mug like a lifeline. "I wasn't sure…" Her voice drifted off.

"Of course." Jenna took in a deep breath and let it out slowly. She'd learned there were times for chitchat and times to get right to the heart of the matter. This was one of the latter times. "Forgive me for being abrupt, Becca, but I'm pretty sure you didn't ask to meet me so we could relive old times. You and I didn't have any old times. I didn't have any with anyone, as a matter of fact. So what's going on?"

Becca began shredding the paper napkin in front of her. "I was in Helena one day and went into the bookstore to get some things for my kids. They had a display for both of your books." She gave a short, rough laugh. "To tell you the truth, I was shocked. I had no idea you had that kind of talent. I don't think any of us expected it—"

"Let's not talk about the past," Jenna broke in. "Let's concentrate on the present. So, you saw my books…"

Becca nodded. "I bought both of them and read them. Then I did an online search and found some of the stories you've done. Investigative pieces. I think what impressed me the most was your fearlessness investigating the cases."

"Becca, did you send me a couple of emails?"

Panic flashed across Becca's face for a moment, then she swallowed and nodded her head.

"Y-Yes. We didn't know what else to do. I talked to the girls about it after I read your books. The fact that you weren't really part of everything made it easier for me to reach out to you."

"The girls?"

Becca nodded. "Y-yes. There's f-five of us. And it happened to all of us."

Shock chilled Jenna's blood. How many young girls had this bastard raped? How many still hid in fear, knowing they'd be killed if they came forward? She forced herself to be calm, because it was important Becca feel safe with her. She reached across and rested her hand on the other woman's arm.

"Okay. Here I am, and I promise you nothing you tell me will go beyond this booth."

Becca glanced over at Scot.

"Don't worry about him," Jenna assured her. "He's a former SEAL. He's most definitely not going to tell anyone."

"Okay." The other woman seemed to gather her courage then leaned across the table toward Jenna. "You have no idea how bad this really is, Jenna. Really bad. Remember Ruth Hartwig? Her daughter was babysitting the little kids at a big house party at one of the huge ranches. She left them alone for a minute in the playroom so she could get some cold drinks from the kitchen. Someone grabbed her in the hallway, put his hands over her eyes and mouth, dragged her into one of the bedrooms, and raped her. And this just happened a couple of months ago."

Becca's hands trembled and she was shredding the napkin even more.

Nausea struck Jenna. "How old is she?" Jenna asked.

"T-thirteen at the time. Ruth says she doesn't know how the kid managed to keep it together for the rest of the party. When they got home, she rushed into the bathroom and was violently ill. It took Ruth a long time to get it out of her. She said the man told her he'd kill her and anyone she told. Ruth's husband was furious. He still wanted to go to the sheriff, but their daughter was so hysterical, he had to promise not to. But that little girl is still a basket case. She won't even go back to school. Ruth is homeschooling her for now and trying to get her to see a therapist."

"Oh, Becca." Jenna gave the other woman's arm a reassuring squeeze.

"But that's just the tip of it. Jenna, he's been doing it for years. He did it to Julie, for god's sake. Your friend. And killed her. You saw the little article. Right?"

Jenna nodded. "I did, but none of the news items were more than a couple of paragraphs. Just the barest details."

"Julie's dad asked the sheriff about it, and he said there's not much interest in anything in an area as sparsely populated as this is. What the hell does that have to do with it? A killing is a killing."

"There's more," Jenna guessed. "Right?"

"Yes." Becca plucked another napkin from the holder and went to work on it. When a group of us got together one night, and Ruth was telling us about it, and how heartbroken she was at what it did to her daughter, it all came out. It happened to three of my friends when they were thirteen or fourteen. We're sure it's happened to other girls in town." She sniffled. "It's been going on for years. I—"

"Take your time."

Becca took a deep breath then went on. "It happened to me, too, my sophomore year in high school. My father does some local work for your— for Roger Holland. We were all invited to the big Christmas party at the ranch."

And there it was, the ranch again. Was there a connection? Who would have been at both parties? God! She remembered that party. She had refused to go there, afraid he would show up again. Instead, she'd hidden in her room with the door locked, while her friend was being raped.

"I thought maybe I'd see you there," Becca went on, "but your mother said you weren't feeling well. I was trying to find your room to see how you were when he grabbed me."

"Becca, I'm so sorry."

Becca shivered. "Sometimes, even now, I can still

feel those big hands on my eyes and my mouth, his big body pressing me into the mattress while he wraps a cloth around my eyes. Nearly suffocating as he presses me into the mattress. For years, I couldn't stand to have a boy touch me. Thank god for my husband. He loved me enough to finally coax it out of me, and then to help me work through the nightmare so we can have some kind of life together."

"Jesus, Becca." Jenna took a deep swallow of her coffee, even though by now it was cold. She knew what Becca had felt. It brought back vivid memories of her own rape.

"It's way past time that I could report it, even if I had the guts to do it, but it's still going on. We have no idea how often because no one's going to talk about it. Nobody reports it anymore because they don't want to end up dead." She stared at Jenna with haunted eyes. "Nine girls over a period of fourteen years have been killed, and who knows how many more have been raped."

"If these were young girls, why didn't their parents push the sheriff to do something about it at the time?"

"Oh, believe me, they have. They're still plenty angry, with the rapist and the sheriff. They want this man found and don't know why Bartell can't accomplish that. It's even happened to a couple of girls visiting friends here. Their families raise holy hell, but nothing gets resolved. The sheriff keeps saying it's someone who shows up here every few years, but if that's so, a stranger would stick out like a sore thumb."

"Unless he has a legitimate reason for being in the area." Jenna leaned forward. "Becca, thank you for sending me the emails."

"I didn't know what else to do. I figured maybe you could come out here, shake some trees, get involved the way you've done with other stories, and make something happen."

Jenna gave a short little laugh. "I think you give me greater power than I have."

"Please." Becca clasped one of Jenna's hands in both of hers. "Ruthie and a few of the others got with me, and we talked about what we could do. I told them about you, so we drew straws to see who would send you the email, and I got lucky. Please, Jenna. Please, please, put your investigative hat on and dig into this. We'll help you all we can. Give you names we know of victims."

"And maybe think of anyone who lives here in the county who is a good candidate for this."

"Ruth thinks Bartell knows who it is and is protecting him because he's the one who keeps the sheriff in office."

Jenna turned her head and exchanged a look with Scot. He'd been quiet all this time, drinking his coffee, resting his arm casually around Jenna to give her his support.

"We wondered the same thing," he said.

Becca looked over at the other diners then back to Jenna.

"We, um, came up with some names that we think might be him. We didn't have a lot to go on since no one has seen him or heard his real voice. This is just based on physical build and who has enough power that they can get away with this. It's a very short list." She fished a slip of paper from her purse and slid it across the table.

Jenna unfolded it and read it, holding it close to her. Five names. The same ones she had come up with. The bank president. The president of the cattleman's association. The representative from their district to the state legislature. The owner of the ranch second in size to Roger Holland's. The president of the State Bar Association. These were all men who were born into wealth and/or power, and their positions had just continued to grow. She had to swallow back the sudden nausea to keep from throwing up on the table.

Which one of them? Who was so evil he would do this, and keep doing it for years?

"We actually brought up a lot more names," Becca went on, "but from everything we remembered, these are the most likely candidates."

"You'll have to be extra careful with this, Jenna,"

Scot interjected. "Just be aware of that. I know I'm repeating what we've already said but I can't say it enough times. Whoever this guy turns out to be, he's very powerful and determined to keep his identity a secret at all costs."

Becca's face turned pale. "Oh, Jenna, we don't want you to put yourself in harm's way. We just thought you were better at digging up facts than we'd be." Tears clouded her eyes again. "We just need to do something."

"But quietly," Scot said in a low voice. "Not in a way that will call attention to what we're doing."

Jenna looked at him. "We?"

"Damn straight. Aren't I your boy friend?" He gave her a tiny squeeze and added in a very low voice, "and maybe a little more."

"Would you be willing to meet with the others?" Becca asked. "Two of the women were raped ten years ago and the others, like Ruth, have daughters who were raped. Two of them, their girls were murdered."

Jenna looked at Scot for guidance.

"I'd say that's a good idea. That way we can get information firsthand. But let me suggest we do this far away from town. Like maybe even one county over. And we should do it soon."

Becca nodded. "I'll call everyone as soon as I get back in my car. I don't want to make the calls from here, even though we're pretty much out of the mainstream. We'll pick a place. If I can get everyone together for tomorrow night does that work for you?"

"The sooner the better," Jenna agreed.

"Why don't we all exchange cell numbers," Scot suggested. "That way we can keep in contact with each other, and Becca, you can confirm the meeting with us."

They took care of it in the booth. Then Scot signaled for the check.

"Thank you again for this," Becca said. "We are all really desperate."

"We'll get it taken care of," Scot assured her.

Becca left first then Jenna and Scot headed out to his pickup.

"Let's go back to the cabin," Jenna said. "I'm going to do some deep research on the residents of this county. See what I come up with. I especially want to dig into Sheriff Bartell's background, see if there are any articles about who his supporters and/or friends are."

"Good idea. I brought my own laptop with me, so I can help you."

She glanced over at him, startled. "You did? You will?"

His lips curved in an unfamiliar grin. "Sure. I'm not just a pretty face."

Jenna laughed, the first real laugh she'd enjoyed

since she received the emails. "You are a surprising person."

"That's right. I'm full of surprises." He reached over and squeezed her hand. "Just remember that."

As soon as they were back in the cabin, Jenna set up her laptop at the little dining table. Scot retrieved his from the bedroom and set up across from her.

"Before we get started, how about some lunch?" he asked. "Those sweet rolls were every bit as good as advertised, but neither of us ate much."

"Oh." She looked across at him, startled. Food was the last thing she'd been thinking about. "Sure. I'll look and see what we've got."

But Scot pushed back from the table and stood up.

"Easier for me. I know what we've got. You need to get to work. That's a better use of your time."

"Wow! A bodyguard, a boyfriend, and a cook all wrapped up in one. How lucky can a girl get?"

The same heat she'd seen before flashed in his eyes.

"I don't know. Maybe you should find out."

He winked—winked!—then moved into the kitchen area.

Jenna stared, doing her best to ignore the unfamiliar flutterings in various parts of her body. The last thing she needed was for Scot Nolan to think she wanted a roll in the hay with him. How could she tell him she had all these hang-ups because she'd never really gotten past the trauma of the rape? Although if anyone could help her, she had a feeling it could be him.

I need to get my act together here and focus on the reason for this trip.

But lord! Scot was making her feel things she'd never expected.

Determined to forget about everything but her project, she opened a web browser and began her research. She had bookmarked the news items about the murders, so she brought them up and made a list of the victims. She thought it strange that there were very few details about the condition of the bodies or how they were found. The only fact listed was that they were all strangled by a man with large hands whose fingers left huge bruise marks on their necks.

Anger, she thought. And rage. How dare these nothings attempt to destroy his life?

Then she began a meticulous search for everything on the names on Becca's list. And for good measure, she threw in Sheriff Owen Bartell.

CHAPTER 7

THE MAN SAT in a copse of trees on a rise that looked down on the cabin where *she* was staying. He knew they'd gone to meet that damn Becca Reiter way out at Eagle's Nest. Having access to countywide information kept him well informed. Then he'd taken a drive out this way and was satisfied they were holed up in the cabin for at least the afternoon. He'd have to figure out what to do after that.

Of all the damn rotten luck. Why did *she* have to come sticking her nose into this? With her writer's nose for information, who knew what she could dig up?

He and the others in their exclusive little club had met to discuss the situation this afternoon. The others had insisted he had to be the one to dispose of her. Not so easy with that SEAL glued to her side. He had to figure out a way, though, or they were all dead.

The whole thing had seemed like good fun when they'd thought it up years ago. They all had skewed sexual appetites, and young girls aroused them the most. The first time he'd forced one of them, he'd hardly been able to believe how excited he got, how hard his cock was and the thrill when he shoved himself into virgin sex.

Jesus!

He'd gotten so excited that when he went home that night he had to get himself off again or risk doing damage to himself.

The others, it seemed, were the same. They met once a month, in their private place, to relive the excitement and share details. And those delicious little girls were too scared to report it. Until one did, and he was sure all holy hell would break loose. Well, they were all threatened with death if they did, so he had to take care of that first one, and he did it himself. And he made sure the investigation went nowhere, despite the anguish of her parents.

But then, almost a year later, another one reported it. The others decided he should take care of her because he'd done such a good job before. And truth to tell, he got off on the killing as much as he did fucking them. Now there were nine total, and he sure as hell hoped there wouldn't be any others. They all agreed they'd remind their new pieces of ass how many bodies there already were.

But now he'd have to get rid of Jenna Donovan. He knew she'd just keep digging until it all came out, and they couldn't have that. He'd have to get rid of that fucking SEAL first, and that was easier said than done. But he was smart. He'd figure out a way. He wasn't about to have his cushy life disrupted by some fucking female.

He knew his chance would come if he was just smart about it. Meanwhile, he sat and watched.

JENNA WAS EXHAUSTED, mentally and emotionally. They'd spent the afternoon doing research, and the amount of information she found on each name was astonishing. These were men who all, including Sheriff Owen Bartell, held positions of power in the area and had for some time. And Bartell lived on a small ranch that, despite its size, had to have cost a pretty penny. He didn't pay for it on a sheriff's salary.

So who couldn't stop the craving for this heinous crime? Who had to be paying Bartell to sweep it under the rug?

She shared her information with the women at dinner. They were shocked that she thought it could be more than one, but agreed if that was the case these were real possibilities. The stories they shared with her about the rapes over the years curdled her blood and brought all those memories she'd suppressed screaming to the front.

Tomorrow, she'd start putting everything into some kind of order. Then she'd write the first of what would be a series of articles about rapes in the Crazy Mountains that had gone on for more than two decades. And she knew just where to submit them. That ought to get some action.

Scot checked everything outside before they walked into the cabin. Once inside, she dropped onto the couch and began massaging her neck. A tension headache was threatening

"I can help you with that." Scot sat down beside her. "I mean, if you're okay with me touching you."

Strangely enough, she was. Throughout the entire day and evening, as she battled with her past and dealt with the danger of the present, she realized how in such a short time his presence had become both reassuring and tempting.

Tempting!

To a woman who'd thought of sex as just something to be suffered through, if she could get up her courage.

"Jenna?"

She realized she'd zoned out.

"Yes. I mean, okay. I—I'd appreciate anything you can do. My nerves are strung tighter than a tennis racquet.""

He shifted her so she was sitting sideways on the couch, between his thighs.

"Close your eyes," he told her in that deep voice that now covered her like a warm blanket and made all her secret places throb and tremble. Places she was sure were frozen yet in less than twenty-four hours this man had begun to thaw them out.

She did as he asked and with his strong fingers he began to work the knots out of her shoulders and neck. Little by little, the tension eased from her body, and the headache that had threatened began to subside. She kept her eyes closed and let herself fall into the feeling.

What if she kissed him again? Would he even want to after she'd pushed him away? He knew what a hot mess she was with the baggage she carried. Why would he even waste his time? But lord! This was the first time in all these years she'd felt actual desire for a man. What if they tried it? But what if she froze?

"Stop thinking." His deep voice smoothed over her. "You're getting all knotted up again."

She drew in a deep breath and let it out slowly. "Sorry. Can't seem to shut off my brain."

"I'm going to ask you a question that is none of my business and very inappropriate, considering our situation."

Her giggle was tinged with hysteria. "Ask away. You know my history. I have no secrets from you."

"Oh, I don't think that's true. I think you have a few hidden away."

"What did you want to ask?"

He put his mouth next to her ear. "Did you enjoy that kiss last night as much as I did? I don't want to overstep here, Jenna. I wasn't all that hot to take this assignment, but I think we have an unexpected connection. If you tell me no, this whole thing is forgotten."

Which she knew was what she should do. But then she thought, what the hell? She wouldn't be any worse off than she already was, the hot mess of the world. And he was the first man she'd wanted in, well, forever.

"Jenna?" He squeezed her shoulders. "Should I take back the question?"

"No. I mean, yes. I mean,…oh, hell. No, don't take it back and yes, I enjoyed it"

"Then how about we try it again?"

When she nodded, he turned her so she was sitting on his thighs, cupped her chin, and drew her face close to him. His pressed his mouth to hers with a light touch, as if waiting to see whether or not she'd bolt. When she didn't, he traced the seam of her lips with the tip of his tongue, back and forth, gentle, again waiting for her reaction.

Unfamiliar heat washed through her and she opened her mouth, welcoming his tongue. Her nipples tingled, and the muscles in her sex clenched with need.

Holy hell! All this from a little kiss?

But there was nothing little about it. It invaded her entire body. When she sucked on his tongue, boldly, he bit down gently on hers. Fire shot through her. She lifted her hands to cup his head, threading her fingers through the silk of his hair. The feel of his beard against her skin was erotic. She could have rubbed her face back and forth over it for hours.

With his mouth still fused to hers, he slipped one hand beneath her sweater and coasted it along her rib cage until he cupped one breast. He squeezed, and she moaned into his mouth. Then he pinched the nipple and without warning, she froze. Everything. Her hands. Her lips. Her tongue.

She felt him draw back at once, and she wanted to cry.

"Don't." His voice was gentle. "If this is as far as you can go, it's all good. We can try again."

"No." She almost shouted the word. "I don't want to stop. I'm so tired of being an emotional cripple. I've let that man steal my whole life, and I want it to stop." She opened her eyes and looked into his. "You're the only man I've ever been able to really respond to. Please don't stop." She bit her lip. "Unless this is too much for you, and I won't blame you if it is. Really. We can just forget this ever happened.

"Only if you want to." He cradled her cheeks in

his palms. "I've had my own hang-ups, Jenna. I closed myself off for so long so I could do what I had to with the SEALs that I wasn't sure I'd ever be able to feel. No one else has ever gotten past that wall until you. And I can have all the patience you need."

Again, it was his words that crumbled her barriers more than his actions.

She looked into those chocolate eyes and smiled.

"Don't stop."

"Okay, then," he whispered and pressed his mouth to her.

He eased his hand beneath her sweater and moved it until he once again cupped her breast. He abraded the taut nipple with his thumb while he stroked the inside of her mouth with his tongue. This time, she moaned and arched up to him.

The kiss went on forever, his tongue exploring, tasting sweeping, while he teased her nipple until it ached with need. He turned his attention to the other one and soon it, too, was swollen and aching.

"How about I take off the sweater?" he asked in the same soft voice.

"Okay," she whispered.

He eased it up and over her head, tossing it to the side. He reached for the clasp of her bra then looked at her, waiting for her to stay stop or go on.

"Yes. Take it off."

He did so, with a gentle movement, and dropped it onto her sweater. Jenna forced herself not to at once cover herself with her arms. This was Scot, the man she'd trusted from the moment she met him. The first man to kindle desire within her. So she sat there, naked to the waist, and let him look his fill, even as she trembled inside.

His brushed a kiss over her mouth again then trailed his lips down the line of her throat to the swell of her breasts, planting little kisses. Then his palms cradled her breasts, and he closed his lips over one swollen tip, sucking it into his mouth.

"Ohhhhhhh." The long cry burst from her at the sensation of fire that raced through her body. Moisture seeped into her panties, and she had to squeeze her legs together against the sudden fierceness of the throbbing there.

Scot lifted his head, a frown creasing his forehead. "Did I hurt you? I can stop."

"Don't you dare," she protested. "Keep doing it. Please."

His laugh had a low, guttural sound that was as arousing as any touch of his.

"Okay, then. Glad to oblige."

He took the other nipple in his mouth, squeezed both breasts as he sucked it into his mouth and grazed it with his teeth. Jenna couldn't believe how hot and needy she was. By the time he lifted his head, she was crazy with need. She had never felt this kind of desire before, never felt her body respond in this way.

Take off your shirt," she whispered, tugging at the shirttails.

He smiled down at her. "Of course."

He tossed it to the side on top of her pieces of clothing, and there he was. Lean, broad-shouldered, muscular, with a dusting of curls on his chest that matched the hair on his head. She ran her fingertips over his pecs, hungry to feel every inch of his skin. She found his flat, male nipples beneath the hair and stroked them with her fingertips. She thought what a good thing it was that she'd read so many romance novels trying to get past her own hang-ups or she'd have no idea what to do.

While she explored his chest and his rock-hard abs, Scot sprinkled kissed over her breasts and teased her nipples until she was nearly out of her mind.

He lifted his head and looked at her. "Doing okay so far?"

"Better than okay," she gasped, as heat consumed her.

"Maybe we could take off a few more clothes?" He put it in the form of a question, which made her like him all the more. He was letting her take the lead. She knew, no matter how much control it took on his part, he'd stop any time she needed to.

"Okay."

He shifted them so she could stand and without waiting for him, she unsnapped and unzipped her jeans and shoved them down her legs. All she had left were her panties, which were utilitarian and about as sexless as you could get. It didn't seem to matter to Scot, however. He stared at them, wetting his lips with his tongue.

"Take them off." His voice was hoarse, and the look in his eyes nearly seared her skin.

Her hands trembled as she hooked her fingers in the waist and eased the flimsy material down her legs. When she stepped out of them, she kicked them to the side and stood before him, naked, shaking, her sex so wet she could actually catch the scent of her musk, a very new sensation for her. Uncertainty crept over her as she waited for him to say something. Maybe he didn't like what he saw. Maybe he was disappointed. For one awful moment, she was tempted to grab her clothes and race up to the loft.

But then he reached out and touched her, running his fingers over her breasts, down her tummy, brushing the curls between her legs. And all the while there was no disguising the approval and hunger blazing in his eyes.

"Beautiful," he said in a husky voice. "Just as I knew you'd be."

"Your turn." Could he hear how shaky her voice was.

Without saying a word, he unbuckled his belt and disposed of jeans and boxer briefs in one swift movement.

Ohmigod! That was all she could think.

He was gorgeous, with lean hips, long, muscled legs, and a cock that could tempt a saint. Thick and swollen and very large, the head was a dark purple, and a tiny bead of fluid sat directly on the slit. She didn't have to ask if he was aroused. It was obvious.

But now what? Could she go through with the rest of it, or would fear take over as it always did? Of course, she had to admit no man she'd been with could hold a candle to this one. Plus, no one had ever taken the time to arouse her and make her feel secure as Scot did.

While she was wondering what to do next, he lifted her and carried her into the bedroom, yanking back the covers and sitting her on the edge of the bed. Then he stood in front of her, his swollen cock front and center.

"Touch it," he said in a soft voice. "Go ahead. It's not going to hurt you, Jenna. And yes, it will fit because we're going to make sure you are good and ready and wanting it as much as I want you. Come on. Put your hand on me."

Hesitant at first, she reached it and wrapped her fingers around his cock. The outer skin was soft, but the shaft it covered was hard as steel. And hot. So warm it heated her palm. She stared at it, fascinated, then touched the little bead of fluid with a fingertip and brought it to her mouth, licking it. It tasted salty and smooth, and she licked her lips. His cock jumped in her hand, giving her an unfamiliar feeling of power.

On impulse, she leaned forward and licked the head then drew her tongue the length of it.

"Better take it easy," Scot said in a shaky voice. "I'm not sure how much control I have left."

"Oh! Am I doing it wrong?"

His laugh had a touch of hysteria in it. "No, you're doing it just right. I wanted you to touch it, feel it, taste it, so you'd know that it isn't a man's cock that hurts you but how he uses it." He lifted her hands, leaned forward, and nudged her so she fell back on the bed. "My turn."

Oh god. Here it comes. Please don't let me scream or push away.

But he had other things in mind. He dropped to his knees between her legs, nudged her thighs apart and traced the line of her slit with the tip of a finger. She shivered at the feelings that consumed her, and deep inside her a pulse began to beat. He traced the wet flesh again and again before he spread the lips of her sex and helping himself to a taste.

The feel of his tongue as it stroked her set her on fire and ignited a need unlike anything she'd ever known or expected to know. When he closed his lips over her sensitive clit, the throbbing inside her sex accelerated. And then he went to work on her, thrusting first one then two fingers inside her and setting up a steady rhythm. Her inner walls pulsed and flexed against his fingers, but then he closed his lips over her clit and sucked, hard, and she exploded. Her inner walls gripped the fingers inside her, spasming against them as tremors rocked her body.

He rode her through the orgasm, licking and sucking and stroking, until the last tremor subsided. She felt so weak she wasn't sure she could lift a hand, never mind move. Scot kissed his way up her belly, between her breasts and to her neck before reaching her lips. She could taste herself on his mouth. A sensation so erotic she could feel her hunger building in her body again, just that fast.

Scot shifted her so she lay with her head on the pillow then went to the dresser and took something out of a shaving kit on top of it.

"I'm always prepared." He grinned, showing her the foil-wrapped condom. He climbed onto the bed, straddled her, and smiling down at her. "So far so good?"

"So far very good."

"Let's see how this goes, because I need to be inside you more than I need my next breath."

He unwrapped the condom, sheathed himself then lifted her legs, draping them over his thighs.

"We'll take this nice and easy. You tell me anytime you panic and need to stop, and I'll do my best to accommodate you."

He didn't know at this point she'd kill herself before she put a halt to this.

She closed her eyes and tried not to grit her teeth as she waited for him to enter her. But instead she felt his mouth on her again, licking her hot core, drawing his tongue through her slit and tugging on her clit with his teeth.

The same intense feelings of desire clawed their way up through her body again. She was so intent on the sensations rocketing through her that she almost missed it when he entered her, slowly, still stroking her clit, easing himself into her a little at a time. It took a moment before she realized he was fully seated in her, every bit of him. When she opened her eyes his mouth was curved in a hungry grin and desire flared hot and bright in his eyes.

"Okay so far?" he asked.

"Yes." The answer came out on a whoosh of breath.

"Okay, then. Here we go, nice and easy."

And that was what he did, taking his time so her body accepted him, rubbing her clit, easing in and out until her sex was so wet that the slide and glide was easy. Then he picked up the pace.

"Ride with me, Jenna. Wrap your legs around me."

She did, locking her ankles at the small of his back, while he took her on a ride so sensuous it involved every part of her body and blanked out her brain. She was aware of the orgasm building inside her again, higher and harder, and of Scot riding her with long, powerful strokes. And then, before she could even get ready for it, the climax burst over her, hot and hard. Her inner walls grabbed his throbbing cock, and her whole body shook.

It seemed to go on forever, and she wondered if she'd survive. Then, suddenly, Scot slumped forward and the tremors eased, as did their breathing.

"Look at me, Jenna."

She did, and was caught up by his warm smile and the emotion in his eyes.

"I—had no idea," she said. "All these years…"

"Maybe you were just waiting for me," he teased.

But she thought, *Maybe I was.*

He sprinkled kisses on her face and brushed them over her mouth before finally easing from her body.

"Be right back."

When he returned, he had disposed of the condom, and he climbed into bed with her, spooning her against his body

"No need for you to climb those stairs tonight," he murmured in her ear.

"I don't think I have the energy, anyway."

He chuckled. "Good."

She was wondering what came next as she drifted off into the best sleep she'd had in years.

CHAPTER 8

JENNA HAD no idea what to expect when she woke up the next morning. Would they be back to business as usual? Would Scot regret what had happened? Should she act as if nothing had happened at all?

But when she awoke and rolled over, she discovered him awake and watching her with a smile on his face.

"Think we chased some demons last night?" He traced a line across her forehead and down over her nose.

"Yes." She wet her lips. "Thank you."

"Hey. I didn't do it for gratitude. I did it because I wanted to. Because I've wanted to feel this way about someone since I left the SEALs, and it didn't happen until you. I was just afraid you weren't going to be able to get past that terrible trauma." He brushed a kiss over her lips. "This may be quick, but it's more than a roll in the hay to me. Please believe that. I want to see where this goes. How about you?"

Relief washed through her. "Yes. Me, too."

"Good. Then let's clean up this mess so we can get on with our lives. I've got some ideas I want to run past Hank. By the time you're dressed, I should have a good outline of what I want to do." The look he gave her was filled with so much emotion and strength. "And don't forget, I'm still your bodyguard. This just makes it that much more imperative that I keep you safe."

He insisted they shower together, where he made delicious love to her. If anyone had told her when she first met Scot Nolan that he would be like this she'd have told them they were crazy. But then she remembered something a friend had told her. "When you meet the right person, there's no timeline, and everything is different."

After he was finished she took a long time washing her hair and rubbing lotion into her body before she dressed. Scot headed into the kitchen to make breakfast. He was just disconnecting a call on his cell when she wandered into the kitchen.

He pulled her close for a moment and gave her a brief kiss.

"Mmm. You smell delicious."

She grinned. "That was the idea. Who were you on the phone with?"

"Hank. I wanted to run something past him and

maybe get his help. Let's sit down, and I'll tell you." He served up two plates of bacon and eggs and filled two mugs with coffee.

Jenna stared at them. "Wow! I might have to keep you around."

He gave her one of his hot looks. "You just might."

"Okay, so give with the details."

"Here's the thing." He took a swallow of coffee. "We could be here for weeks talking to people and trying to shake something loose, and truthfully, I wouldn't mind that at all. But I think it's time to bring this to a head. Those women are still terrified, and people are scared for their teenagers."

"So, what do you propose?"

"We need to force someone's hand, and the most likely person is the sheriff. I'm sure he's covering for whoever this is and will keep doing this until the guy is too old to do this anymore."

She nodded. "I agree."

"I don't like the idea of using you as bait, but I'll have you well protected. Hank wasn't all that happy about it, but he agreed we need to make something happen. He's sending a couple more agents to help me."

Jenna frowned. "Help you with what?"

"We're going to stir the waters a little. Becca said she'd set up appointments for you to talk to some of the other women, and to those who are older now but wow were raped as teenagers. Let's call her to set them up today and tomorrow."

"Okay, but how does that move things along?"

"You're going to tell Sheriff Bartell what you are doing and ask him if he wants you to pass along to him anything you learn."

Jenna's eyebrows flew up. "Are you kidding?"

"Not in the least. Tell him you're also planning to take pictures of a couple of the places where the bodies were found. Becca and the others were pretty specific about the locations last night. Tell him which two you're going to, and that you just wanted to inform him in case anyone noticed what you were doing."

"And if he gives me a hard time?"

"He can try all he wants, but you are free to interview people for a story. You can even hint to him that you might pick up a clue or two, if he's interested."

She took a sip of her coffee then set the mug down. And where will you and Hank's men be all this time, my personal bodyguard?"

"I'm going to be driving you to your appointments. Hank's men will be stationed at both murder sites." He paused. "The tricky part is separating us so you go out there alone."

"Wait, wait, wait." Her stomach did a flip-flop. "I don't think I can buy into that. I'm finally agreeing with everyone that I need this kind of protection."

"We came up with a plan that we think will work.

When you call Bartell, ask him if those two places are hard to find, because I'm not able to go with you and you don't want to get lost."

Jenna frowned. "You think he'll buy it? He'll probably tell me to just say away from those places. They are crime scenes. Of course, I can point out to him the crimes were a long time ago and I'm free to take any pictures I want."

"I'm sure he will, but you'll tell him you are going anyway."

"And where will you be, my faithful protector."

He grinned. "Under a blanket in the back of your SUV. You don't think I'm letting you go five feet without me, do you?"

Some of the tension eased from her. "Good."

He reached for one of her hands, a serious expression on his face. "Jenna, when I left the SEALs, I was ready to find someone and build a life with them. But that was two years ago, and I'd begun to think it wasn't going to happen. That I wasn't able to make a connection with someone like I wanted to."

"I hear a but in there."

"But then I met you, and it didn't take long for me to feel the connection I wanted. I don't know if you—"

She reached over and pressed her fingers against his lips. "I didn't think I'd *ever* be able to have a relationship. That rape kept me traumatized all these years. And then you came into my life, and, well, now I'm really hopeful."

"After this is over, can you take some time so we can really see where this is going?"

"I can and I will. I feel as if my life has been on hold for as very long time and someone just pressed my Go button."

Scot's smile curled her toes. "I'm happy to push your buttons anytime at all."

She blew out a breath. "Then let's get this done."

Becca was more than happy to set up the appointments for her.

"They will be thrilled to talk to you," she assured Jenna. "I'll call you back as soon as it's all confirmed."

Sheriff Bartell wasn't quite as happy about it. His reaction was just as Scot predicted—irritated, aggravated, and pissed off.

"I told you before, you need to not stick your nose in this. These people have been through enough."

"But don't you think they deserve answers?" she persisted.

"They'll get answers when I find them," he snapped.

He was even more angry when she told him about the pictures she planned to take.

"Those spots are crime scenes. Stay the hell away from them."

"They aren't recent crime scenes," she pointed

out. "And I'm sure other people have traipsed through them."

"I don't need reporters screwing around with my people and my county. I'll handle the cases. You should go back where you came from. Stay the fuck out of my county."

The phone slammed in her ear.

"Well." She looked at Scot. "That's one unhappy camper."

"If he had nothing to do with this, I'd think he'd be glad of any help at all."

"Makes you wonder, right? Well, let me get my tablet and notebook, and we can get going." She shivered. "I'd like to get this over with as soon as possible. Like I said that first night, I didn't realize how much being back here would depress me."

He leaned over and brushed a kiss over her lips. "I'll do my best to help you get rid of that feeling. Come on, now. Let's get going."

The interviews went well, all things considered, even as emotional as they were. Ruth Hartwig broke down and cried and had trouble pulling herself together. She said her daughter was still seeing a therapist. Two other women had the same reaction, but then the last two Jenna met with were more angry than depressed and said they'd do whatever it took to help her find answers.

"It's depressing how many lives this selfish, arrogant man has ruined," she told Scot. "Just for his own selfish reasons."

"I could kill him and not lose a moment's sleep over it," he said. "Hopefully Bartell will have passed the word along about your interviews and visits to the sites. You ready?"

She drew in a deep breath to settle herself, let it out, and nodded.

"Let's do it."

They drove back to the cabin to pick up Jenna's SUV. Then, just in case anyone was watching, they drove off in their own vehicles, meeting up outside of town after they were sure no one was watching them. Scot had found a place to stash his truck. Then they put the seat down in Jenna's SUV, he climbed in, checked his Glock 19, and curled up beneath a blanket.

She pulled away, having set the location on the GPS on her phone, and followed the directions. She hoped whatever happened took place at her first stop. Not that she was anxious for the confrontation. More to the point, she wanted to just get it over with. Catch whoever showed up, make him tell if Bartell was involved, and turn everything over to the state police, which was what Hank had told Scot they'd do.

The spot she came to was a heavy grove of trees along the side of the road, one that went several yards back. It was isolated, on a highway without much traffic. And where it would take days, as it had, for the body to be discovered. She parked in a space between some of the trees, grabbed her phone, and headed into the woods. Many of the trunks were thick enough to conceal someone, so she looked carefully around as she walked to the small clearing where the bodies had been found.

She had just started taking pictures when she heard a twig snap behind her and turned to find Sheriff Bartell standing there, a look of rage on his face. He grabbed her camera with one hand and her hair with the other.

"You just had to stick your fucking nose in my business, didn't you," he growled.

He was pulling her hair so hard, Jenna had to stand on tiptoe to relieve the pain.

"Whoever you are covering for deserves to be revealed and arrested. Rape is one of the worst crimes you can commit."

"It's not a crime if you enjoy it." The look on his face chilled her blood.

"I hope whoever this is pays you a lot of money for all the lives they've destroyed all these years." Scot's voice was edged with rage. " Now, let go of her damn hair."

The sheriff released her, and Jenna stepped far away from him, rubbing her head.

"You still don't get it, do you?" Bartell asked. "It wasn't just one person. It was six of us. Yes, us," he added when she gasped. "We all had the same cravings. It's how we took our pleasure all these years."

" But you won't be taking it anymore." Like a ghost materializing out of nowhere, Scot appeared behind Bartell and shoved his gun in the sheriff's back. "Let go of her hair if you don't want a bullet in your spine."

"You won't pull that trigger." Bartell's voice was edged with bravado.

"Don't bet on it. I was a sniper with the SEALs. I killed bad guys for a living."

"And so did I." Another man appeared from the trees. "Scot, keep your gun on him while I truss him up. Then we'll toss him in the back of the truck and haul him to the highway patrol. Their headquarters is in Helena, and Hank's already contacted them so they're expecting us."

They frog-marched Bartell to the other agent's pickup, but before he tossed him in, Scot got up close and personal with him.

"Without you and your playmates exposed. I'd venture to say a lot more people will be coming forward."

"They'll keep their fucking mouths shut or else," Bartell spat.

"Or else what? A real law officer will be taking statements now. This whole disgusting game just fell apart."

"You ready now?" the other man asked Scot.

"I am. Oh, and Jenna? Say hello to Charlie Zero."

"Sorry we had to meet like this," Charlie said. "Scot, you help me get this asshole tied down real good in the truck before I take off. I'm going to call Hank so he can have the highway patrol send a car to escort me. You take your lady home. She looks like she's had a quite a day."

"Hi, Charlie." She was proud she'd managed to keep herself together. "Thanks for helping."

"It's what we do."

Jenna managed to keep herself together while Charlie drove off and then when Scot followed her back to the cabin. But once inside, she collapsed on the floor, and the tears she'd been holding back for years fell as if they'd never stop. Scot picked her up off the floor and sat on the couch with her on his lap, holding her against his chest and murmuring soothing sounds to her.

They sat that was for a long time as she burrowed into his warmth and the safety of his arms.

It was dark out by the time her emotions finally settled down. Scot insisted on giving her a hot shower and bundling her in her thick robe. Then he made her some hot soup, and a cup of tea liberally laced with bourbon.

"We won't talk about this anymore tonight," he ordered. "I want to help you sleep. Then, tomorrow, we'll find out what's going on. Okay?"

She nodded, apparently incapable of speech.

And that was what they did. He held her in his arms until she finally drifted off to sleep, for once without nightmares.

"IT'S A NINE DAYS' wonder," Scot said as he disconnected a call on his phone. "Apparently Bartell tried calling his friends to have one of them get a lawyer for him. When everyone hung upon him, he decided to see what kind of deal he could get if he gave everyone up."

"So there really was a group doing this? Not just one man?"

Scot nodded. "Bartell was cozy with the others—the ones you thought might be involved, by the way—and in civilian clothes handled security at their big parties. They were sitting in someone's den after one of the shindigs. Someone—no one wants to admit who—complained about his wife being an ice cube and wouldn't it be great to get a taste of young flesh for a change."

"So they thought it would be wonderful to have this good-old-boys club raping virgins so they could get their rocks off?" Jenna thought she might throw up.

"So it seems. People like that make me sick."

"Who killed the girls who came forward?"

"The highway patrol thinks it was Bartell. They

found the pictures of the dead girls with fingerprints on their neck and they're comparing them. Can you believe he kept those pictures all these years?"

"I can believe anything at this point," she said in a sad voice.

"Hank will keep us up to date over the next few weeks as things unfold. And he's hoping you'll do not just a series on this but also another book. Get the word out, so to speak. Let other women and girls know how dangerous men who abuse power can be."

"I had that in the back of my mind. But what I'd really like is to put all of this away for a couple of weeks and just enjoy finally being free of that nightmare."

"Funny you should say that." He carried a mug of fresh coffee to the table for her and sat down next to her. "Hank asked me if I'd like a couple of weeks off after this, even though it was a short stint and not really taxing."

Her heart did a double-time beat. "And what did you tell him?"

"I told him I either wanted to take someone sight-seeing in the Crazies or sit on a boat in Florida on the Gulf of Mexico." He grinned. "I guess that depends on which you like better."

She stared at him. "You want to spend it with me?"

"Didn't we say when this was over we'd see where it could go?"

"Yes, but—" She bit her lower lip.

"But you weren't sure I meant it?"

She nodded.

"Jenna. I've never meant anything more. I feel the kind of connection with you I've been looking for the past two years. Are you all in?"

"Yes." She laughed. "Yes, I am. So where do we start? Montana or Florida?"

"We can talk about that later. I know where I want it to start right now."

He picked her up and carried her to the bedroom, pulling her down on the bed with him.

And then there was no more talking.

HIDDEN DANGER

DESIREE HOLT

USA Today
Bestselling Author

Turn the page for a taste of Hidden Danger, my first
book for Brotherhood Protectors

BROTHERHOOD PROTECTORS

HIDDEN DANGER

DESIREE HOLT

USA TODAY
BESTSELLING &
AWARD-WINNING
AUTHOR

CHAPTER 1

I'M GOING to make him sit down and listen to me. If this was a mistake, I need to know that now and move on. Maybe that's what I get for grasping at straws.

With that whirling in her mind, Alix Bonner exited the interstate and turned onto the two-lane highway that led to the ranch-style mausoleum she called home. Her stomach was knotted with a combination of anger and anxiety. She had hoped the weekend at the Vanity Fair Spa would relax her and help her put her life in perspective. But nothing had been able to push the thoughts out of her mind that had been spinning around there since her whirlwind marriage to Lee Bonner.

What's wrong between us, Lee? I wanted to use this weekend to find out. Why has business suddenly become more important?

He had been so edgy the past couple of weeks

she'd had to tiptoe around him. Something was wrong, and she was determined to find out what it was. Her plans to stay home this weekend and try to work this out between them were torpedoed when Lee announced he had business meetings. She was beginning to get sick of all the damn business meetings. When was there time for the two of them?

After the first week of their hasty marriage, she had the feeling Lee had relegated her to the sidelines. The only thing he seemed to have time for with her was hot sex, which wasn't so hot anymore, and to show her off at dinners and events with business people. He was generous with money, but she was beginning feel as if he'd bought and paid for her. And she had no idea why. Something was very wrong, but she had no idea what it was.

And, yesterday, he'd been particularly uptight.

"Couldn't we spend the weekend doing something together?" She pressed her palm to his cheek. "Maybe it could relieve some of your stress."

"Not possible. This is important." Then, as if it occurred to him he might be angering or upsetting her, he wrapped his fingers around her wrist and moved her hand. "Maybe next weekend, okay? For now, go to the spa. Enjoy yourself. Spend the weekend there."

She was still trying to decide if he'd been encouraging or just trying to get her out of the house.

When her cell phone rang, she checked the

screen, hoping it was Lee telling her his meetings were over. No such luck. Not Lee, but Gina McMasters, her closest friend in Houston.

"Hello, lady of the manor." Gina's voice was bright, as usual. "How goes life in the mountains?"

"It's not exactly in the mountains, but close."

"Just checking up on life with the gorgeous hunk."

Gina had been there when she met Lee at a hotel event and probably would have run away with him herself if she'd been the one he had his eye on.

"Life is...fine." She put a deliberate smile in her voice. "It's great, in fact."

Liar.

"Better than Houston," Gina pointed out.

"Yes," she said. No way would she let Gina know what her situation had turned into. "Much better. Listen, I have to go but I'll call you later, okay?"

"Alix? You okay?" Concern edged Gina's voice.

"Yes. Fine. Call you later."

She thought she'd had a nice life in Houston, with a great job as event coordinator at one of the major hotels and a relationship with what she'd thought was a great guy. If the sex wasn't off the charts, so what? Maybe her expectations were too high. Then the roof fell in on her. A mega chain bought the hotel, and someone was brought in to replace her. She'd had her eyes on the prize, but the new owners took the prize away. How stupid she was not to have seen that coming.

And Barry, the long-term relationship she'd invested so much in, had given her a shock she still couldn't fully accept. She'd wanted to kill him when she discovered he was one of the attorneys handling the hotel deal. And that the deal had been in the works for two years, and he'd used their so-called relationship to get as much inside information as he could. Talk about feeling like the village idiot. It didn't say a whole hell of a lot about her ability to pick a man, or about her intelligence.

She had to recognize the fact that Lee Bonner had swept into her life at a low point, dazzled her, and waltzed her into a hasty wedding. But now it appeared like he was strike two in her choosing-a-man department. What had happened to her brain? Her smarts?

Maybe she should have a T-shirt that said *Stupid*.

She turned onto the highway leading to their house outside Eagle Rock.

Almost home.

She knew money wasn't the problem with Lee. Generous was too mild a word for her husband. But the situation at home had niggled at her from the minute she'd left the house yesterday. Had she made a mistake falling into this whirlwind marriage? Was he sorry, now, after barely three months, that he'd married her? The thought nagged at her more and more.

She'd begun to wonder if all Lee had been

searching for was a great hostess for the parties he loved to throw and an acceptable wife on his arm for the events they attended. When had everything begun to deteriorate? Was she even in love with him anymore? Had she really ever been, or had she just anxious to get out of Houston?

Maybe she needed to find a job to occupy her when he was gone so much on business. How would Lee react to that? And was there even a place in Eagle Rock that could use her skills?

Shut up, Alix. Just find him and make him listen to you. If he won't, you'll have to think about walking away. Start fresh someplace else.

She glanced at the dashboard clock. Three o'clock. At first, she'd thought about calling him from the spa, but she was afraid he'd tell her to stay there. Just going home was better. When she got there, she'd call his cell, hoping he answered, and coax him into coming home early. He didn't like her calling when he was involved in business, but that was tough. This was important. She wanted answers, and she wanted them now. But as soon as she turned into the long drive, the knots in her stomach tightened even more. Several cars were parked in the turn-around in front of the house. Lee never had business meetings at home, especially with this many people.

She drove carefully around to the side of the house, surprised to see the garage door open as she pulled into her slot. Leaving the weekend bag she'd taken with her in the back seat, she entered the house quietly, surprised at the silence that greeted her. Then she heard the faint murmur of voices coming from Lee's den, which he liked to call his cigar room. It was where he indulged in the hand-rolled Cuban cigars that were frequent merchandise on some of his trucks.

Should she go knock on the door? Sit in the kitchen? Find something to do until whatever this gathering was ended? Lately, Lee had been so on edge, she often had no idea what would set him off.

She took a tentative step into the living room... and stopped dead. The giant flat-screen television set was on, but the image paused on it didn't come from any television show, she was sure. Instead, it held a montage of pictures of men's faces or their bodies. The men in some of the pictures were obviously dead, and not so neatly, either. In the others, there was just a head shot, but she wouldn't want to meet any of them on a dark night. Beneath each photo was the word *Eliminated* or *Set up for Elimination*.

This couldn't be some television show. The image was static, unmoving on the screen. Then she noticed the light for the DVD player was on. What kind of disc had something like this on it, and where had it come from? What did Lee have to do with it?

For a moment, she was frozen in place, shocked. Panic surged through her, making her heart rate triple. Her stomach roiled, and she had to bite her lip to keep from throwing up. What in god's name was Lee involved in? Why would he be killing people? He had a trucking empire that had made him uber wealthy. How did all this figure in? Did any of this explain Lee's increasingly strange behavior for the past three months? And who were the men he was closeted with?

The boom of laughter sounded faintly in the den, and someone said in a loud voice, "Killing those fuckers was a pleasure."

Oh, god. Oh, Jesus.

She needed to get the hell out of here before anyone knew she was home.

Please don't let me pass out. And don't let me make a sound. If they find me, will they kill me, too?

Then a tiny part of her brain kicked in.

A record. Make a record of this.

She pulled her cell phone from her purse, her hands shaking so badly she almost dropped it, and snapped a couple of pictures of the television screen. She was so panic-stricken she didn't notice the spa receipt she'd stuffed into her purse fell onto the floor. As quietly as she could, she eased into the garage and climbed into her car. She prayed silently that the noise of the engine as she cranked it would not penetrate the thick walls of the house. She gave fervent thanks the garage was on the opposite side from Lee's den.

Heading down the driveway, she forced herself to

maintain a low speed to minimize engine sound. But when she turned onto the highway, she hit the gas, and the car leaped forward. And fear leaped into her throat again. She kept checking her rearview mirror, terrified she'd been heard and Lee or someone would follow her. If they caught her, she'd be as good as dead. She knew it.

What the hell is going on? Who were all those people marked Eliminated? *What am I going to do? Where can I go?*

Her hands were shaking so badly she worried she'd steer the car into a ditch.

She was pretty sure the bodies in the pictures were of dead people. What was Lee doing discussing dead bodies with whoever was at the house? Who was this man she'd married, that he could discuss killing people while smoking cigars? And who were the men with him?

Then another thought stabbed at her—Lee would call the spa this evening. Wherever he was, whatever he was doing, he always called her at nine o'clock at night. For a long time, she thought how nice it was that he wanted to chat with her no matter where he was or what he was doing. Now, she wondered if he was checking up on her. But why? That heart-stopping scene in the living room was giving her an instant case of paranoia. How had she gotten herself into this situation? Lee Bonner had been so attentive, affectionate, and caring when he'd swept her off her feet and out of Houston. What had gone wrong? Or had she just not seen the real man?

Forget the pity party and quit acting like a fluff ball. You have more important things to think about.

Wasn't that just the damn truth? She wasn't stupid by any means, although she was beginning to think her marriage to Lee Bonner gave the lie to that. But easier said than done. *Okay*, she told herself. *Think. think. think.* Like where she could go, and whether Lee could find her there. And what she would do after she got there, wherever *there* was. She gave fervent thanks she had cash with her. It was a habit she'd developed a long time ago, and one she was thankful for now. The only clothes she had with her were the ones she'd packed for the spa. Damn. But that still didn't give her a direction to take.

She had gone about ten miles from the house and was nearing the little town of Eagle Rock when her engine began making a weird noise. She eased up on the gas a little then fed it slowly, but the noise only increased. Then, with a loud pop, it stopped altogether, and steam or smoke seeped out from beneath the hood.

No, no, no!

The tears she'd been fighting off now ran down her cheeks, and she pounded the steering wheel in a combination of fear and frustration. What was she supposed to do out here in the middle of no place, where she'd be ripe pickings for Lee and his men?

She was pretty damn sure she'd have to call the garage in Eagle Rock for a tow, and that would leave a trail for Lee to follow. Normally, she'd be dialing his cell phone, or calling the house for Frank, who'd apparently been with her husband forever and lived in the little house behind the big one.

After what she saw back at the house, however, that wasn't an option. She didn't know who she could trust. She needed a place to hide, a mechanic for the car, and someone to help her. Right. With no resources to call on. Crying wasn't going to give her any answers.

Her hands shook as she pulled out her cell to scroll through the numbers, hoping one would pop out at her. But everyone listed was either connected to Lee or miles away. When she heard the sound of a car coming up behind her, she froze. Would it stop? What should she say? She looked in the rearview mirror and, sure enough, there was a black SUV pulling up right to her bumper.

Oh, god. Is this someone Lee has sent? Does he know I was in the house after all?

She couldn't decide if she wanted him to try to help her or keep on going. Making sure the doors were locked, she watched the driver get out and walk up to the car. She wiped the tears from her face with the back of her hands and did her best to pull her fraying edges together, gripping the steering wheel so he wouldn't see how badly her hands were shaking.

The loud knock on the window made her jump.

ALL CHARLIE ZALMAN, better known as Charlie Zero, wanted to do was go home, take a hot shower, grill a steak, and veg in front of the television. He had just completed a month-long bodyguard job for Brotherhood Protectors, one that had taken every bit of energy to complete. Some people were just more difficult to protect, and, often, they were the ones who needed it the most.

Some days, he longed to be back in the SEAL teams, but then a twinge in his right arm reminded him of the metal pins that would always be part of his body and resulted in the medical discharge that left him a civilian. He'd lost a good friend in that firefight, too, a loss he still struggled with, wondering if he could have done anything different.

But the hospital stay and the end of his SEAL career had been only some of the bad news waiting for him. Someone should have warned him that when the woman you thought was waiting for you said, "I'll always be here," she actually meant she'd be there until someone better came along. Someone with a sound body and no bad dreams.

He gave thanks daily, however, for Hank Patterson, the former SEAL he'd gone to high school with who had started the agency and was more than happy to bring him on board. The agency became the entire focus of his life, helping him effectively blot out those things he wanted to forget. If now and then he wished for someone in his bed, he always reminded himself his good right hand was ever faithful.

He had been dreaming of the shower and the steak when he nearly ran into the silver sedan half-on, half-off the road, blocking traffic in one lane.

What the fuck!

Casting his eyes heavenward in a *Give me strength* silent plea, he climbed out of his vehicle, made sure his T-shirt was untucked to cover the gun at the small of his back, and jogged up to the driver's door of the sedan. The woman sitting behind the wheel might have made his tired cock sit up and say *Take me out to play* if he wasn't so fucking tired and she didn't look like one big mess. Masses of dark hair that looked as if she'd been running her fingers through it surrounded a face with high cheekbones and eyes so brown they reminded him of pools of chocolate. Her full lips were bare of any lipstick, but Charlie didn't think she needed any. The T-shirt she wore with bling scattered over it probably cost as much as his entire outfit. Which, he thought, wasn't hard. It also fell softly against small but full breasts that he—

Jesus Christ, Zero. Put your cock away and see what's

going on here. This woman gives every appearance of being in some kind of trouble.

It pissed him off even more because no woman had had that instant effect on him for a long time.

Great. Just fucking great.

She was sitting with her fingers gripping the steering wheel so hard he could see the whites of her knuckles even through the glass. Either she was oblivious to his presence or ignoring him, so he rapped on the window. She jerked up straight, hard, as if she'd been shot. But she kept her eyes focused straight ahead, so he rapped again, wondering if she could grip that wheel any tighter. What the hell was going in there? Who got that tense over a car breakdown?

"Hello?" He didn't want to shout and scare her half to death, but he couldn't figure out why she was ignoring him. "Hey! We need to get your car moved before someone rams into it."

That got her attention. She turned her head and lowered the window a couple of inches. Crap! Were those tears tracks on her cheeks? He wondered if her skin was normally that pale.

"What?"

Oh, great. Another idiot. At least this one wasn't related to someone they owed a favor to.

"Your car." He did his best not to growl at her. "It's blocking the road. You have to move it. What's wrong with it, anyway?"

When she wet her lips and gripped the wheel again, he began to get the feeling she wasn't just an idiot but someone with a real problem. He studied her through the window and an itch crawled between his shoulder blades. This woman was in a panic about something, and her obvious fear of him went beyond what she might feel for a stranger on the highway.

Good going, Charlie. You always get the women in distress.

"I...It just conked out. Steam came out from beneath the hood, and I'm not sure I know what to do about it. It won't start now."

Charlie swallowed a sigh. "Let me check it out and see if I can figure out what's wrong. Hit the hood release button."

For a brief moment he worried she might not know where it was, but again, he didn't think she was stupid. Just scared. And getting more frightened by the minute, as evidenced by the glances she kept stealing over her shoulder.

"Are you looking for someone?"

"Y-No. No, I'm not." She wet her lips. "Do you think you can fix the car?"

"Let me check it out." But one glance under the hood told him this wasn't a roadside repair job. The motor was a damn mess. This baby needed a tow. "I hate to be the bearer of bad news, but you need to call the garage in Eagle

Rock for a tow. This is beyond a quick roadside fix."

Her face turned whiter than his sheets. "But I can't— I mean, I don't—"

Charlie waited, but she just sat there, biting her lip, fear growing in her eyes. He wanted to ask her what the hell was going on, but he was pretty sure she wouldn't tell him.

He sighed and tugged his phone out of his jeans pocket. "Listen. I know the county sheriff real well. How about if I call him, and he can vouch for me. Then maybe I can get you some help." He paused. "Whatever kind you need."

He could see her debating the situation. Again, he wished to hell he knew what she was so frightened of that even calling the sheriff was a problem. Was she running from the law? She sure didn't appear as if she was, but Charlie well knew that looks often lied.

Then her shoulders slumped. "I guess that would be the smart thing to do. But I'll call the garage myself. You can go on to wherever you're going."

"At least let me push you fully onto the side of the road. Someone's going to come along and clip you, otherwise."

"I— Okay. What should I do?"

"Put the gearshift into neutral. I'll do the rest."

As soon as she nodded, she raised the window again. He gave a mental shrug, put his muscle into it, and managed to get the car enough off the asphalt so nobody coming by would knock into her. Then he rapped on the window one more time and motioned for her to lower it. Taking a business card from his wallet, he handed it to her.

"You call Sheriff Tate. Ask him about us." He turned the card over. "That's my cell number on the back. If you decide you need any kind of help with… whatever, just give me a call." He paused. "And don't wait too long to make those calls. This might be peaceful territory, but you never know when trouble can come along."

"Thank you." She whispered the words, but the expression on her face was more fear than gratitude. Again, she glanced behind her, checking the road for vehicles.

What the hell?

He cleared his throat. "This is none of my business, but if someone's out to hurt you, maybe I could—"

"No!" The word was almost a shout. "No, please. I-I'm fine."

She sure didn't look fine. He'd have been irritated if not for the sheer panic on her face. He got the feeling she was almost as afraid of him as she was whoever or whatever she was running from. "Okay. I'll be on my way."

As he pulled out onto the asphalt and drove toward his house on the other side of Eagle Rock, he couldn't get the woman out of his mind. That itch between his shoulder blades was stronger, but it was an itch he couldn't scratch because he had no idea what the fuck was causing it. He just couldn't get rid of a bad feeling he had about the whole business.

He'd noted her license plate in his cell phone. When he got home, he'd call Hank and ask him to use the setup in the office to do a search. See who it was registered to. Hank might even know the owner. Even though Charlie had also grown up in the area, he didn't have his finger on everyone's pulse the way Hank did.

He was barely at the edge of Eagle Rock when his cell rang. The number on the readout was unfamiliar. He hit the button to accept.

"Zero," he barked.

Silence.

"Hello? Anyone there?"

"Um, is this the man who pushed my car off the road?" The voice was faint and more than nervous. Just plain scared, he'd say. "It says here your name is Charles Zalman. Is that you?"

Did she think he handed out cards with fake identification on them?

"It is. Change your mind?"

He waited through a brief pause, wondering if she'd hung up. What the hell was with her, anyway?

"Yes. Can you come back here right away? I-I think I'm in trouble."

Of course she was. Besides the obvious signs, did he know anyone who wasn't?

He pulled out his calm, reassuring tone of voice. "I'll be right there. Stay in your car with the doors locked like you were. Hang on. I'm on my way."

But first, he texted the license plate to Hank with a request to see who it was registered to.

There were no cars on the road other than his, so he made a wide U-turn and hit the gas, pushing the speedometer past eighty. He passed a couple of cars coming from the other direction. He wondered if any of them had stopped and how the woman had handled it.

Then he was there, making another wide turn so he could pull up right behind her. He jogged up to the driver's side of her car, and there went his antennae again. She was still sitting in that same rigid pose, as if relaxing would cause her to fall apart. Her face was even whiter, if that was possible, her hands clenched into fists in her lap. When he rapped on the glass, she jerked as if hit with an electric wire. She opened one hand to lower her window.

"Did you call for a tow?" was the first thing he asked.

She shook her head. "No. I... Just... No."

"All right." He swallowed his questions and pulled out his cell. "Let's take care of that first."

Charlie felt marginally better when Reggie Forman said he'd head out right away. He stashed his phone and turned back to the woman. "We'll wait for him, but—"

"Wait for him?" If possible, her face grew even paler. "Can't we just go?"

Charlie lifted a brow. "Go where? And we have to give him the keys."

"We could drop them off. I—" She swallowed. "I really want to get out of here."

She was doing the checking-over-the-shoulder thing again. Yeah, definitely spooked.

"Okay." He made his voice as low and even as possible. "Come on. Get out of the car and bring the bag in the back seat with you."

She stepped out of the car and reached for her bag. Her hands trembled so much it almost fell from her fingers. Charlie took it from her, gently, and guided her into his SUV. She couldn't have been much over five feet and, at the moment, looked extremely fragile. She also had the faint scent of some kind of flowers clinging to her, tantalizing him and making his hormones dance.

Fuck!

"Hold on a sec," he told her and went back to grab her car keys from the ignition. Then he called Reggie. "He's okay with us leaving them at the garage," he told the woman. He said he's almost here, anyway. Do you have someplace I can take you? Anyone who can provide transportation or whatever?"

She shook her head. "No." Her voice was so soft he had to strain to hear it.

"Do you know *anyone* around here?"

She bit her lip then, after a long moment, shook her head. "No one I can go to."

Wasn't it just his damn luck? Charlie swallowed a sigh then punched another number on his cell.

"Hank? Hey, it's Charlie. Yeah, I was headed home but change of plans. I'm bringing a guest to the office. The woman who belongs to the license plate I sent you. She's spooked by something and has no place to go. Maybe we can help."

Hank chuckled. "Another stray?"

Charlie ground his teeth. It was a joke among the agents that he drew strays like magnets drew metal. He chose to ignore Hank's comment.

"We'll be there in twenty."

"See you then. Oh, and by the way, something very interesting came in while you were still gone. Something I'll want you to be part of. This is a Zero specialty."

"Okay." A sour taste filled his mouth. Hank's words meant whatever this was had to do with guns and drugs, two things Charlie had a personal reason to hate.

"You sent him my license plate?"

He felt the fear rolling off the woman next to him in heavy waves. "Professional habit. In our line of work, you learn to check everything about everyone you come in contact with. You never know what might come back to bite you in the ass."

"And now you're taking me someplace. I—" She stopped. Let out a breath. "Can you tell me where we're going? Are you kidnapping me?"

If the situation didn't have danger written all over it, Charlie might have chuckled.

"Look." Charlie made his voice as gentle as possible. He had much experience with skittish women, unfortunately. "You said you have no place to go. It's obvious something's scared the crap out of you. You saw that card I gave you. Brotherhood Protectors is a group of former special forces military who work to help and protect people. I can assure you we're all safe. If someone's after you, there's not a better group to take care of you. And maybe you'll feel safe enough to tell us what this is all about. Okay?"

"Okay." She gave one sharp nod of her head.

"You know my name. How about telling me yours?"

She was silent for so long, he wondered if she would tell him.

"Alix," she said at last. "With an I."

"Well, Alix with an I, I'm taking you someplace where you'll be out of harm's way. Then maybe you'll feel safe enough to tell me what's got you so spooked."

The Brotherhood Protectors' office was in the basement of Hank and Sadie's new house, just outside Eagle Rock. There might even be a couple of other agents there, too, prepping for new assignments. He hoped to hell they didn't scare the woman beside him. She was strung so tight, he thought almost anything might set her off, and the Protectors could be intimidating.

He wondered just what kind of trouble this woman was in. And how the ever lovin' hell he'd explain this to Hank.

ABOUT DESIREE HOLT

USA Today best-selling and award-winning author **Desiree Holt** writes everything from romantic suspense and contemporary on a variety of heat levels up to erotic, a genre in which she is the oldest living author. She has been referred to by *USA Today* as the Nora Roberts of erotic romance, and is a winner of the EPIC E-Book Award, the Holt Medallion and a Romantic Times Reviewers Choice nominee. She has been featured on *CBS Sunday Morning* and in *The Village Voice, The Daily Beast, USA Today, The (London) Daily Mail, The New Delhi Times* and numerous other national and international publications.

Desiree loves to hear from readers.

www.facebook.com/desireeholtauthor
www.facebook.com/desiree01holt
Twitter @desireeholt
Pinterest: desiree02holt
Google: https://g.co/kgs/6vgLUu
www.desireeholt.com

www.desiremeonly.com

Follow Her On:

Amazon
https://www.amazon.com/Desiree-
Holt/e/B003LD2Q3M/ref=sr_tc_2_0?
qid=1505488204&sr=1-2-ent

Signup for her newsletter
http://eepurl.com/ce7DeE

facebook.com/desiree01holt
twitter.com/desireeholt

ORIGINAL BROTHERHOOD
PROTECTORS SERIES

BY ELLE JAMES

Brotherhood Protectors Series

Montana SEAL (#1)

Bride Protector SEAL (#2)

Montana D-Force (#3)

Cowboy D-Force (#4)

Montana Ranger (#5)

Montana Dog Soldier (#6)

Montana SEAL Daddy (#7)

Montana Ranger's Wedding Vow (#8)

Montana SEAL Undercover Daddy (#9)

Cape Cod SEAL Rescue (#10)

Montana SEAL Friendly Fire (#11)

Montana SEAL's Bride (#12) TBD

Montana Rescue

Hot SEAL, Salty Dog

ABOUT ELLE JAMES

ELLE JAMES also writing as MYLA JACKSON is a *New York Times* and *USA Today* Bestselling author of books including cowboys, intrigues and paranormal adventures that keep her readers on the edges of their seats. With over eighty works in a variety of sub-genres and lengths she has published with Harlequin, Samhain, Ellora's Cave, Kensington, Cleis Press, and Avon. When she's not at her computer, she's traveling, snow skiing, boating, or riding her ATV, dreaming up new stories. Learn more about Elle James at www.ellejames.com

Website | Facebook | Twitter | GoodReads | Newsletter | BookBub | Amazon

Follow Elle!
www.ellejames.com
ellejames@ellejames.com

facebook.com/ellejamesauthor
twitter.com/ElleJamesAuthor

Made in the USA
Lexington, KY
10 January 2019